Solomon's Riches
The Way to True Wealth

Steve Darr

Solomon's Riches © 2021 by Steve Darr. All rights reserved.

Published by Author Academy Elite
PO Box 43, Powell, OH 43065
www.AuthorAcademyElite.com

All rights reserved. This book contains material protected under International and Federal Copyright Laws and Treaties. Any unauthorized reprint or use of this material is prohibited. No part of this book may be reproduced or transmitted in any form or by any means, electronic or mechanical, including photocopying, recording, or by any information storage and retrieval system, without express written permission from the author.

Identifiers:
LCCN: 2021907808
ISBN: 978-1-64746-777-7 (paperback)
ISBN: 978-1-64746-778-4 (hardback)
ISBN: 978-1-64746-779-1 (ebook)

Available in paperback, hardback, e-book, and audiobook

All Scripture quotations, unless otherwise indicated, are taken from the Holy Bible, New International Version®, NIV®. Copyright © 1973, 1978, 1984 by Biblica, Inc.™ Used by permission of Zondervan. All rights reserved worldwide.

Any Internet addresses (websites, blogs, etc.) and telephone numbers printed in this book are offered as a resource. They are not intended in any way to be or imply an endorsement by Author Academy Elite, nor does Author Academy Elite vouch for the content of these sites and numbers for the life of this book.

This is a work of fiction. All of the characters, organizations, and events portrayed in this novel are either products of the author's imagination or are used fictitiously.

DEDICATION

I dedicate this story to those who continue to look into the rearview mirror of their life, dragging their past with them instead of forging forward with renewed strength, wisdom, and zest for life.
A different life is possible.
Your thoughts become your reality.
Know you are magnificent.

A friend loveth at all times,
And a brother is born for adversity.
—King Solomon
Proverbs 17:17

TABLE OF CONTENTS

FOREWORD IX
THE BREWING STORM XI
A DAY AT THE MAILROOM. 1
HEADLONG INTO THE STORM 7
WHAT AM I GONNA DO? 15
BAD NEWS. 19
END IS NEAR. 25
AFTERMATH AND DEBATE 33
DECISIONS, PLANS, AND PREPARATIONS 41
STRANGER IN A STRANGE LAND. 51
RESCUE 57
THEIR ADVENTURE BEGINS—THE DIG 63
DISCOVERY. 73
TREASURE. 79
INTO THE DEPTHS 85

THE TRUE DISCOVERY	95
REVELATION	109
RECONCILIATION	115
TRUE WEALTH	131
RETURN AND DEFEAT OF THE SHADOWS	141
A NOTE FROM THE AUTHOR	147
ACKNOWLEDGMENTS	151

FOREWORD

By Geoff J Gardner Ph.D. (Retired)

I had the pleasure of meeting the author, Steve Darr, when we joined the same online marketing company. We hit it off immediately as colleagues. Soon after, we became friends despite our geographical distance—Steve is in the USA, and I am in the United Kingdom.

Steve freely gives his knowledge, experience, and time. He is a very humble person.

Currently celebrating his seventh decade of life, he is prepared to release his first novel.

By chance, Steve asked me to write this Foreword. During one of our frequent talks about our stories and experiences, he learned I am a published author. What a privilege and honor to contribute and be chosen by a man and a friend I hold in high esteem to write this.

As an author, I know how important it is to support your family and friends through the publishing process. I am more than happy to give my friend, author Steve Darr, my support.

Steve's desire in writing this novel is to tell the story of a young man who, after living a life of believing lies and blaming his circumstances, realizes *his* thoughts are at the root of his situation. With the help of his childhood friends, a minister,

SOLOMON'S RICHES

and a mysterious archaeologist, he realizes the consequences of his thoughts. Through unforeseen circumstances during a faraway journey, the three friends learn about themselves, their friendship, their desires, and discover the meaning of true wealth.

The author brings his main characters to life through their varying emotions: anger, rage, devotion, drive, love, happiness, and ultimate success.

What more can we ask for in a story brought to life purely from the mind of one man, Steve Darr.

—Geoff J Gardner
Dr. / PhD. Retired
Author: *The Black Colonial*
www.theblackcolonial.com

PROLOGUE

THE BREWING STORM

At 6:10 p.m. on a Tuesday, Pete and Mary Ann Tobias sat at the dining table in the craftsman bungalow where Pete grew up. As they ate dinner, Mary Ann saw the depth of Pete's fury as he picked and jabbed at his food in silence. She felt a storm brewing as she gazed at the third place setting at the table.

He said, "I can't believe he can be so inconsiderate and thoughtless! How many times have I told that kid—what—a hundred times over the past twenty-three years? He knows what time we have dinner around this house!" Pete slammed his fork down and ripped the napkin out of his lap. He pushed his chair back and crossed his arms. "It's as if he is directly defying me!"

Mary Ann pointed her fork at him. "Listen, he's a young man. He isn't a kid anymore. Besides, I don't understand why you get so riled up at him for being late for dinner. He has a life. He and his friends are probably out at the Grotto playing video games and relaxing after work. You know they've been like the three musketeers since they were children. They're the only *real* friends he has. No doubt, he's probably lost track of time."

"Lost track of time? That's precisely my point; he doesn't have anything but thin air between those ears of his. He couldn't care less about anyone but himself, and he's been that way since the day he was born!"

Mary Ann rolled her eyes in exasperation. "Oh, for heaven's sake, you aren't going to start on that again, are you?"

"Well, you know it's true. You knew I never wanted a kid in the first place. But right out of high school, you got pregnant, so I had no choice but to support the three of us. But twenty-three years later, here we are—*still*."

Mary Ann was horrified. "I can't believe you're saying these things! You're his father, for heaven's sake!"

"Well, he should be out on his own. He's lazy and never made anything of himself. Plus, he didn't even apply himself in school and did only mediocre work!"

"You know that wasn't his fault, and it wasn't *laziness*!" Mary Ann slammed back, defending their son.

"Yeah, yeah, they figured out he had some learning disability after high school. Big deal—it is just another excuse! I still think he's a little bit stupid." He rolled his eyes.

"He's *not* stupid! His brain works differently. Remember how great he was at solving tricky puzzles? He proved the kids wrong when he solved the Rubik's Cube in *eighteen seconds*—the other kids bet he couldn't do it in twenty seconds! I was so proud of him and loved the look of surprise on those kids' faces when he did it!" She nodded at the memory.

"Yes. He should go *real* far with *that* talent! I'm certain the information will impress employers as they read his resume. You're making excuses for him again." Pete stood up and paced back and forth like a caged animal as Mary Ann sat there speechless. "He needs to get his head out of the clouds. Why can't he buckle down and make a man of himself rather than being tied to his mother's apron strings?"

She thought she might scream. Instead, she picked at her food and thought of her next words to defend their son. But before she could speak, Pete continued.

"All you do is mollycoddle him! A minute ago, you said he wasn't a kid anymore; he'll never grow up unless you stop making excuses for him and treating him like a child. You do *everything* for him! And you have no idea the trouble I had to go through to get him that job working in the mailroom at the mill." He glared at her and raised his arms in exasperation.

She stopped eating, stood up, and leaned across the table toward him. With every ounce of constraint in her voice, she said, "Oh, yes, I do. You make a big issue of it all the time, and frankly, I am sick of hearing about it!"

"Well, I hoped it would at least give him a start, but already, they've said how he comes in late sometimes, shows no interest in the work, and continually makes mistakes. What brains does it take to work in the *mailroom?*"

"Exactly, what brains *does* it take to sort mail and copy documents? It's no wonder he's bored and doesn't take an interest in the work! And wait, what's this? You have someone spying on him and reporting back to you?"

"I want to make sure he's doing a good job. The quality of his work reflects on me!"

She crumpled back into her chair, exhausted from yet another argument about him. "Pete, do you still love me? Did you *ever* love me?"

"Of course, I love you. I've *always* loved you. Why would you ask such a question?"

"Because there are times—like now—when I feel like you blame me for making your life miserable because I got pregnant with him. And there weren't—well, *we* didn't take the proper precautions."

"No! No! I wasn't ready to be a father and never wanted to be a father. You knew that!"

"Why? Because of *your* father?"

"No, not because of him. I wanted it to be the two of us, that's all."

"I just thought—because he was so horrible to you. . ."

"It all happened too quickly. We were kids in love, and then *bam*, we were parents. Everything changed. He was the focus of your love and affection, and I was—and still am—nothing more than the breadwinner around here."

"You really feel that way?"

"Don't think for a moment I don't still wonder what our life together might have been like without him," he said matter-of-factly.

"Are you jealous of him?"

He turned to her and leaned on the table with sad, angry eyes. "Yes! Yes! *Yes!* There, I've said it! Are you happy now? You've always cared more about him; it's never been the same between us since he came into our lives. I hoped it would change once he got older, but it's worse. He's twenty-three years old, still lives in the basement, and doesn't have any reason to make something of himself because I keep a roof over his head and food on the table. And you do *everything* for him! He's downright lazy, a loser! The kid is never going to make anything of himself."

She sat in disbelief over his words. Frozen to her chair, she whispered to herself, "His name is Jonathan."

Pete turned. "What?"

"His name is Jonathan. I said his name is J-O-N-A-T-H-A-N! You can't even bring yourself to say his name!" She cried softly into her napkin.

He continued to rant as if she hadn't said a word. "I'm trying to make a man of him, and you continually make excuses for him, his laziness, and lack of a backbone." He slammed his fists down on the table, ratting the dishes.

The sound jerked her from her daze.

"If you weren't so harsh with him, calling him names—*stupid, lazy, a good for nothing*— and constantly correcting him over *everything* he says and does, I wouldn't need to try and *encourage* him."

"He's never going to grow up to be a man without correction and instruction. How else will he learn to do the right things? The way he comes home late for dinner is a perfect example of what I mean. He knows when to be home but still doesn't make an appearance until *he's* good and ready. It's plain inconsiderate and downright discourteous to you!"

Pete snatched up his fork and pointed it at her aggressively. "He acts as if he can just walk in here whenever *he* feels like it and doesn't take any responsibility for himself! I can't abide it, and he's going to hear about it when he finally waltzes through that door."

At that moment, the front door burst open . . .

ONE

A DAY AT THE MAILROOM

Jonathan Tobias worked in the mailroom at Murdock's Paper. His nerdish and baby—yet handsome—face made him look nineteen. He was of average height and build, kept his mousy brown hair uncombed, and usually, his shirt was partially untucked. His boss, Mr. Jacobs, always complained about his appearance. He heard it a hundred times. "Why, can't you look presentable in the office, Jonathan? Try to be more professional, Jonathan." *Blah, Blah, Blah!*

He looked up at the clock on the wall and grumbled about the three hours left before he got off work.

At that moment, Mr. Jacobs walked into the room with a stack of documents. "Daydreaming again, Jonathan? Drop whatever you're doing! The department heads need these before the staff meeting tomorrow morning, so don't dilly daddle. We need these delivered by the end of the day. Get moving *now*! Your father went to a lot of trouble to get you this job—you don't want to disappoint him."

"Yes, sir, I'll get right on it."

Mr. Jacobs dropped the stack of documents on the desk and promptly walked away. Before he left the room, he gave Jonathan one last glare.

As he began the deliveries, Jonathan sighed. *Just what I need today, another stupid thing to do. Now, I have to drop everything and deliver documents when I already have a ton of stuff to finish before quitting time. I hate the way that jerk talks to me and treats me like I'm stupid. He's like all my previous bosses! My dad gives me attitude at home, and I get attitude at work too. What does it take to get a halfway decent boss? They're all clueless, one way or another. Why can't I ever seem to catch a break?*

Jonathan dropped an envelope on a desk and headed to the next one, mumbling to himself, "Ow. Ow. Ow. My legs and back are killing me, but if Jacobs finds me sitting, he'll write me up again—for *laziness*—and if my dad finds out, I'll be in trouble. I want to do something, *anything*, to make Dad happy and show him I'm not the loser he always says I am."

Jonathan's cellphone rang. He recognized the caller ID; it was his friend, Mark Atkins.

"Hey, buddy, how ya doin?"

"Hi, I've been better."

"What's wrong?"

"Oh, I was hoping to get out of here on time today, but ole man Jacobs just walked in and dumped more work on me. I have to get it done before I can leave today."

"That's a bummer. Well, do you think you can meet at The Grotto after work? We can try a couple of levels of that new adventure game. I heard Kevin got it in, and I'm anxious to give it a try."

"That sounds great and gives me a reason to get this stuff done to get out of here on time. Is Kate going to be there?"

"Yeah, I already spoke to her, and she plans on meeting us."

"Great, we'll have a chance to try to start breaking the code to get to the lair before I have to get home for dinner."

Jonathan forgot about his frustrations at work and daydreamed about cracking the game's code with Mark and Kate.

A DAY AT THE MAILROOM

His time with them was one of his favorite things, and he enjoyed solving the challenges of a well-designed game.

Before he knew it, it was 4:00 p.m. As he finished the last tasks, he wondered if other people also daydreamed during work.

Mr. Jacobs sudden presence jerked Jonathan back to reality. "Did you get everything done, Jonathan?"

"Yes, sir, Mr. Jacobs. I took care of everything."

"How about those documents? Did you deliver *all* of them?"

"Yes, sir, they're all delivered."

"It's a good thing you took care of that; you can leave for today, but make sure you get here on time tomorrow. You were late yesterday morning, and I saw you coming in at 8:05 a.m. today. If it happens again this week, I'm going to dock your pay."

"Yes, sir." Jonathan grabbed his laptop bag, walked past Mr. Jacobs, then ran excitedly to The Grotto.

The Grotto, a funky storefront on Main Street in Harrington, was a great place to congregate with friends and other video gaming nerds. It lived up to its name; the gaming area's darkness glowed with the greenish light from the computer screens. It gave the room an aura of a cavern shrouded in mystery. The giant red dragon in the front window was a giveaway to what awaited inside. Jonathan loved the place; it was his kind of environment, and he felt comfortable with the people who hung out there.

He spied Mark, his all-American friend with perfect hair, blue eyes, and a handsome smile. Lovely Kate sat next to him, a beautiful young woman with shiny, shoulder-length auburn hair and a smile that warmed Jonathan's heart. The three of them were close friends. They sat in their usual spot on the couch with their laptops already open, exploring the game.

Jonathan and Mark met when they were five; he lived two doors down the street. Kate joined the threesome when they were all in first grade. He couldn't remember why, but it seemed natural for her to be part of their lives.

"Hey, guys! What's goin' on?"

"Great," Mark added. "I see you got everything done at work to make it here on time."

"Yeah, ole man Jacobs was satisfied, so he let me leave on time. But things with him didn't go well today—not that they ever do. Did I ever tell you he stands outside his office at 8:00 a.m. every day waiting for my arrival? Today, he threatened to dock my pay if I am late again this week."

"Really? What a jerk!" Mark grumbled.

Anyway, how are my two fabulously successful friends doing? How'd your days go?"

"Well, I have a big test on Friday, so it's been busy," Kate responded.

"Oh, that sounds like a lot of fun—*not*! How about you?" Jonathan nodded in Mark's direction.

"We had a pretty busy day at the law firm. I spent most of the day preparing briefs and the research for one of the lawyer's upcoming criminal case."

"*Well*, aren't *we* Mr. Special and important paralegal!" Jonathan retorted, resentful that his friends caught the good breaks with their supportive parents and cushy jobs.

"Aww, knock it off. Let's get on with the game. I am ready to take you on, Dragon Lord!" Jonathan chuckled at their use of nicknames. Mark was the Dark Revenger, and Kate was the Light Healer.

The three friends went into battle against each other in the game. They laughed and cheered one another on as they tried to figure out how to gain points in the fast-paced game. Through the laughter and good-hearted jabs at each other,

A DAY AT THE MAILROOM

they thoroughly enjoyed each other's company as they played the game.

After a while, Mark said, "Hey, I'm getting hungry! Why don't we go across the street to The Dragon and get some carry-out?"

Startled, Jonathan looked up from the game and asked, "What time is it?"

Kate looked at her watch and replied, "It's early, only a little after 6:00 p.m. Why?"

Jonathan felt sick to his stomach, and his face turned sheet-white. "Oh, my gosh!"

"What's wrong?" Kate asked.

"Dinner is at 6:00. My dad is going to kill me. I have to get out of here and get home. Sorry to have to rush off, but I'm in *major trouble*!"

"You're twenty-three years old and worried about being a few minutes late for dinner?" Mark asked.

"Yes, you don't know what he is like if I'm late for dinner!"

Jonathan packed up and rushed out of the building like his feet caught fire, bumping into other gamers, making a loud commotion, disregarding everything and everyone in his path. His only goal was to get out that door and home as fast as he could. He instinctively knew what would be waiting for him when he arrived.

As Mark watched Jonathan clumsily leave, he remarked offhandedly, "Man, I don't know what's going on with him."

"How long have we known him?" Kate asked.

"As long as I can remember, it's always been the three of us. Why?"

"My point exactly. Have you ever known Jon to be any different? He's always had one issue or another with his father. He is terrified of him. I mean, isn't that why we make it a point to encourage and support him?"

"Well, it seems he has gotten worse as we've gotten older. He complains about everything and blames his father—or whoever else bothered him that day—for his troubles. I don't know what to say to him. By the way, what was that wisecrack he made about my job? What was *that* all about?"

"Yeah, that was weird. Sometimes, I think he's a little jealous of you. I mean, it's not the first time he's said something along those lines."

"Jealous of *me*? Why would Jon be jealous of me?"

"Isn't it obvious? You've already graduated from college and work at *the* major law firm in town. He's working in the *mailroom* at the mill because his dad got him the job."

"Jon is my best friend. I don't think he's got a jealous bone in his body."

"Don't be too sure about that. I love him, too, but sometimes, I wonder what's going on with him," Kate said.

"Better be careful letting that slip . . ."

"What slip?" she asked.

"Loving him . . ."

TWO

HEADLONG INTO THE STORM

Jonathan bounded up the front steps of their home, skipping every other one. He burst through the front door and found his father at the dinner table, fork in hand, and shouting in yet another argument with his mother. Before he even entered the room, he knew the fight was about him because the air felt charged with electricity like before a summer lightning storm. When they spotted Jonathan, there was a brief moment of silence.

"Well, it's so nice of you to *finally* make an appearance for dinner; why don't you come right in and have a seat?" Pete said as he waved his fork toward Jonathan's seat at the table.

Jonathan walked toward the dining room. "I'm sorry, Dad. We were at The Grotto playing video games after work, and I lost track of time. I'm sorry, Mom. No doubt you spent all afternoon cooking. I should have been here on time for dinner."

"Yes, you better apologize to your mother. After all the things she does for you—washes your clothes, cleans, picks up after you, cooks—you are *the* most inconsiderate person I have ever known, an absolute disgrace. I'm embarrassed to call you my son. What does it take for you to get it through your head—you need to start accepting some responsibility for yourself!" The veins popped out on Pete's neck. His face was red, and his bubbling anger was evident in every word. "How difficult is it for you to keep track of time and show up here on time for dinner? What does it take? For heaven's sake, you're twenty-three years old. It's pretty ridiculous you're still playing video games like some kid!"

"Lots of adults play video games, Dad. They aren't only for kids. Ours challenge our minds, teach strategies, and winning gives us a deeper sense of accomplishment than a kid's game would. Plus, it's fun playing against each other. We just relax and have some fun." Jonathan hoped explaining the evening to his dad would help him understand.

"You three are still playing silly childish games like you did when you were eight-year-olds! At least *they're* making something of their lives."

"That's unfair. I've tried, but it is hard finding a decent job in this town when I didn't graduate high school and only have a GED," Jonathan said, helpless.

In a tone that dripped with sarcasm, his dad said, "Oh, *you poor thing*. If you had applied yourself in school and made some effort, you'd have a *real* high school diploma. You're *lazy*. Face the fact! You're a *lazy, good for nothing* living in my basement. I'll still be supporting you when you're an old man. But since you're living in my house, you'll live by my rules, and that means dinner is at 6:00. Now, get out of here; get out of my sight. Slither back down to your hole in the basement, and play some more video games," Pete yelled and pointed to the basement door with his fork.

Mary Ann stood up. She rested her left hand on the table, leaned forward, and pointed at Pete. With a furious look on her face, she spoke for the first time since Jonathan entered the room, "I think *that's enough*, Pete. He understands it's important to be home in time for dinner. He'll be more conscientious from now on and get here on time, won't you?" She turned and looked at Jonathan.

Jonathan sat there, shocked. He had never seen his mother raise her voice to his father and didn't know what to make of it.

"*Enough, Enough*, Mary Ann! You stay out of this. This is between *him* and *me*."

She pointed her finger awfully close to his face. "I *won't* stay out of it, Pete. You need to *calm down!*"

"Well, he needs to *grow up*; he's twenty-three years old and needs to start acting like a man."

Jonathan got up from the table without saying another word and went to his room in the basement. He laid on his bed and stared at the ceiling in silence for a few minutes.

Then, he sat up on the side of the bed and reached in his bedside nightstand for his journal. It was a plain, black notebook, but he journaled often, and in doing so, found it helped him handle his awful job, cruel father, and unfair circumstances. He began to write.

Man, today was rough. Jacobs lectured me as usual and insisted I deliver envelopes before closing time. It was great getting to spend time with Mark and Kate. It helped me put the horrible day behind me. Then I was late getting home for dinner!

Holy cow. That was worse than I expected. How could Dad go so ballistic when I was twenty minutes late for dinner? I've never seen him that angry, and I don't like how he talked to mom. He can scream at me all he wants, but he shouldn't speak to her like that. It wasn't her fault. I've got to get out of this place and away from him. But how? My bank account doesn't have enough money saved up right now to support myself. How can I possibly live under his tyrannical rule anymore? Am I really stuck living here until I can figure out what my next move might be?

Just then, Jonathan heard the familiar message chime come from his cellphone. It was a text from Mark.

How did it go when you got home?
Not well at all. Do you have time to talk on the phone?
Sure, give me a call.

He dialed Mark.

"So, tell me what happened."

"My dad went *ballistic*; I have never seen him so angry. It was *so* bad. I was scared he'd have a heart attack or something. His face was so red, and he balled his fists as if he'd punch something—*maybe even me*. He waved his fork around like a sword and looked like some character from a cartoon, which would have even been funny if he hadn't screamed at me so violently. It scared the hell out of my mom and me. I don't get it—twenty minutes late for dinner, and he *freak*ed out. It's time to get out of this house and away from him. But at the same time, I also want to do something special—*be someone special*—so he'll be proud of me. Does that sound screwed up or what?"

"Yeah, but I get what you mean, though. But understand something: you don't have to *prove* anything to anyone. The only person you need to prove anything to is yourself."

"I wish I could do *something* right to make him happy. It's like I have some dark cloud over my head, and everything I touch falls apart."

"Well, you've had your share of troubles, but maybe the job at the mill will work into something good!"

"I wouldn't be too sure about that."

"What do you mean?"

"Well, I had to distribute a set of envelopes to all the department heads today. Mr. Jacobs made a big deal about the timeline, saying I had to deliver them before quitting time for some big meeting in the morning. My curiosity got the better of me, and I took a look at the contents of one of the envelopes." He swallowed, remembering the moment he snuck a peek inside the envelope. "It looks like the mill might be closing in a few months if the company can't get some additional financing or restructuring. The place is about to go under unless something happens soon."

"Maybe that's why your dad got so upset with you tonight?"

"I don't know. The word might have gotten out already; I'm not sure. If the mill has to get rid of people, I'll be one of the first ones to go. My dad will be furious if I lose this job; I don't know what I'd do."

Mark interjected, "Ah, he might have to worry about losing his job, too, if that place closes down. Wow, I wonder what would happen to the economy here if the mill closes?"

"The economy? Really? I have more immediate concerns right now! This house is a living hell for me—a time bomb waiting to go off. I walk around like I'm living in a minefield, waiting for the next explosion."

"Well, how long do you think it will take to get enough saved up to move out?"

"I don't know for sure. Though I have several hundred saved up, I'm sure it is going to take a couple grand to find a place."

"Maybe you can pick up another part-time job on the weekends to supplement what you're making at the mill."

"I don't know. My whole world is upside down right now; I can't think straight after what happened during dinner. He really scared me! Sure, my dad always had a temper, but he was over the top tonight. I think I better play it cool and stay out of his way."

"True. Take it easy and follow all his rules for a few days. Maybe he'll calm down and not be so hard on you. Why don't the three of us put our heads together tomorrow and try to figure some way for you to get out and into an apartment?"

"That's easy for you to say. You've got a good-paying job and a place already. As I said, all I've got is several hundred saved up."

A gentle knock on Jonathan's door jerked him out of his frustration. "Hang on a sec, Mark." He put the phone down and opened the door. "Mom?"

"I brought you something to eat, honey."

"Thanks, but I'm not very hungry anymore."

"Try to eat something. I'll let you get back to what you were doing. Good night."

"Night, and thanks." He kissed her on the cheek.

"Sorry. Mom wanted to make sure I was okay."

"Look, calm down, and try to get some sleep tonight. Get to work on time tomorrow. We'll meet up after work. Say we meet at The South End Café and put our heads together to see if we can develop a plan? We should be able to figure something out."

"Okay. I'm not very hopeful. But thanks. I'll talk to you tomorrow after work."

The following day, Jonathan got ready for work and made sure his father had left before he went upstairs. He greeted his mother in the kitchen with a kiss on her cheek. "Morning. How are you doing after last night? Are you okay?"

"Yes, honey, I am fine. It took your father a little while to calm down, but everything is fine now. Please be sure you're home for dinner on time tonight."

"You can be certain I'll be home in plenty of time for dinner!" Jonathan replied.

"Sit down, honey. Have your breakfast and visit with me for a few minutes before you have to leave."

Jonathan looked across the table and noticed the dark circles under her eyes. "Mom, I'm concerned. You look tired, and you have dark circles under your eyes. Are you *sure* you're okay?"

She reached across the table and touched his hand to reassure him. "I'm feeling a little worn out this morning. Honestly, I didn't sleep well last night, probably because of all the excitement."

"Are you *absolutely* sure you are alright?"

"Yes, son, I am *fine*, just a little tired."

"Well, give me a call if you need anything, Mom. Hey, can I tell you something?"

"Why, of course, honey."

"Dad scared me last night. I'm afraid of him and what he might do to you or me."

"Oh, Jonathan, don't be silly! You know your father has a temper, but he would *never* harm us. Now, you better get on your way. You don't want to be late for work. Your father has someone spying on you."

"Yes, I know."

"You do?"

"Yes, Mr. Jacobs, my boss." He looked at the clock and pushed his chair back. "He'll be watching for my arrival." He grabbed his coat and headed back to kiss her cheek, and said, "Bye, mom!"

He rushed out for work. *I sure hope Mom is all right. She hasn't looked well for the past couple of weeks. I wonder if something is going on . . .*

THREE

WHAT AM I GONNA DO?

Jonathan arrived at Murdock's Paper ten minutes early, ready to work. Mr. Jacobs tried to look casual as he stood in the hall by his office door, but Jonathan knew he was out there to monitor Jonathan's arrival.

"Good morning, Mr. Jacobs. How are you today?" Jonathan called down the hall.

"I'm fine, Jonathan, thanks for asking." Then, as usual, his boss disappeared into his office. Jonathan smiled as he entered the mailroom.

The hours passed slowly, but Jonathan was determined to make a go at his job in the mailroom, even if it bored him to tears. As he continued to sort the incoming morning mail, he contemplated his life. *I don't see any future at the mill, and I will never get out of this mailroom. It all started with school and the lousy teachers who didn't like me, called me a problem student, told me my work was wrong, and I was stupid. The issue was I didn't understand what they wrote on the board, and the reading assignments seemed foreign to me. Tests were awful because I already knew my grade would be a big fat F! And I hated the kids. They always teased me and called me stupid.*

It wasn't until after they kicked me out of high school that they figured out I was dyslexic. But the diagnosis didn't change a thing. I hate being called stupid, and I hear it enough from my father. So, here I am in this crummy mailroom sorting and delivering mail. Is this the only future I have to look forward to—crummy, low-paying jobs, living in my parent's basement, barely surviving in this small town? I gotta get a break; something good needs to happen for me! Jonathan angrily stuffed mail in the appropriate boxes, looked around at the boring mailroom, and rolled his eyes. *Even the wallpaper is boring,* he thought.

At the end of his shift, Jonathan breathed a sigh of relief. He met up with Mark and Kate for coffee and put their heads together regarding Jonathan's situation. The South End Café was a popular coffeehouse for locals. It had a comfortable, inviting, laid-back atmosphere. Everyone knew everyone else there, and Jonathan, Mark, and Kate met there some weekend afternoons. He grabbed a coffee and sat down with his friends.

Mark said, "Okay, you said you have several hundred saved up, so how long would it take you to save a couple of grand?"

"Holy cow. Well, on my salary, that would take months!"

"So, how many months?"

"I don't know, probably eight months, *at least.*"

"Really?"

"Yeah. I don't make the kind of money you make, *Mr. Paralegal.* I haven't been lucky enough to have the breaks you've had and parents who gave a crap about me!"

Mark sat back in his chair. "Okay, don't get yourself all riled up and defensive. I'm only trying to get an idea of your finances so we can figure out a budget to help you put more away."

"Thanks, but I don't think probing into my finances is going to make a lot of difference."

"Well, then, how do you plan to get enough money together to move out if we don't talk about your finances?" Kate added.

"Listen, I don't have dear old mom and dad helping me pay for my college education like you do!"

WHAT AM I GONNA DO?

"What!" She stood up and leaned across the table, getting in his face. "No, you listen, Mr. *High and Mighty*. My parents *aren't* helping pay for my education! I've taken out student loans in my name, and I work two part-time jobs to pay for my education. That's why it's taking me a little longer than usual. And to be clear, we've been listening to you complain about your father and your life for years. We've done everything we can to encourage you and give you our support, but all you've done is complain and blame everyone else for what's happened to you. It's time you start *listening* and *doing* something instead of *complaining* and *blaming*!" Kate sat back down and crossed her arms.

Jonathan grabbed the edge of the table with white knuckles and leaned forward. "What the hell? I thought you were my friend, Kate. You sound like my father. Neither of you knows what it's been like for me!"

"Yes, I am afraid we *do* because you've told us over and over about how miserable and helpless you are because of your dad, the teachers, past bosses, and your *bad breaks*. I've known you since first grade, and Mark knew you before that. We're your best friends and care about you."

"Doesn't sound like that to me. You're as critical as everyone else!"

Jonathan stood up. "I think this conversation is over. It's time to get home for dinner. I'll talk to you guys later." He gathered his belongings and stormed out, letting the door slam behind him, which startled other customers.

Kate banged her fists on the table. "Oh, at times, he infuriates me. He is so pigheaded. Doesn't he realize we're only trying to help? I have an idea to help him, but I have to talk to my dad about it first. Dad has something in the works—it might be the answer for all of us."

"Well, I'm at a total loss, Kate. So, I'm all in for whatever your plan might be."

FOUR

BAD NEWS

Jonathan arrived home and immediately went to his room. He sat at his desk with his face cupped in his hands for a moment, and then he grabbed his journal from its drawer.

What the heck just happened? That ended up being one screwed-up mess! How did I manage to turn a meeting intended to help me turn into a screaming match between, of all people, Kate and me...

I don't get it; Mark and Kate believed this was all my fault. They don't understand what my life is like! We have known each other for years, and I thought they understood me and my miserable life.

The conversation continued to bother him.

Suddenly, a loud noise upstairs jolted him from his thoughts. Jonathan bolted up the stairs and found his mother on the kitchen floor; his father was with her.

"What's wrong, Dad?"

"I'm not sure; she just collapsed to the floor. I think she may have fainted."

"Is there anything I can do? Should I call an ambulance?" Jonathan asked.

"I already have; they should be here any minute."

"What happened? What's wrong with her?" Jonathan pleaded, terrified.

"Aren't you listening? *I don't know!* When I got home from work a few minutes ago, I came in here to the kitchen, and she turned to say something and collapsed!" Pete shouted.

"I told her she looked tired and not well this morning when I left. But I told her to call me if she needed anything."

The wailing sound of an ambulance siren grew closer. Jonathan and Pete watched helplessly as the crew loaded an unconscious Mary Ann on the stretcher.

∞

Pete and Jonathan followed the ambulance to the hospital. "I hate hospitals! Oh, please don't let it be anything serious." Jonathan looked at his dad, hoping for reassurance.

"Shut up! Sit there and be quiet! I don't need to listen to your whining right now!"

They rode in silence the rest of the way to the hospital, and as they sat in the emergency waiting room, they barely spoke. Jonathan hated the sterile, antiseptic hospital smell. He remembered the last time he sat in a hospital waiting room when he was seven, and his granny was sick; she never came home. He fidgeted nervously in his chair, and Pete glared at him.

One of the emergency room doctors approached. Pete and Jonathan stood up to greet him. "Mr. Tobias, I'm Dr. Lawrence. Your wife is awake and okay. But she needs to rest. We would like to keep her for a couple of days so we can run some tests and keep her under observation."

What's wrong with her, Doc?" Pete asked.

"We aren't certain right now. But we will run more tests."

"So, you can't tell us anything?"

"I'm afraid not right now. It's too early to make any determination without more tests. I encourage you to go home for now. We'll move Mary Ann upstairs into a regular room soon, and you'll be able to see her tomorrow."

On the way home, Jonathan asked, "What do you think is wrong with her?"

"I don't have any idea, and if you ask me that question one more time, you're going to find yourself walking home." Pete banged his fist on the steering wheel. "Now, shut up about it." With that, Jonathan sat quietly for the remainder of the trip home.

Two anxious days passed while Mary Ann was in the hospital. Pete and Jonathan visited her, and she seemed in much better spirits. While Jonathan was at work, Pete visited when the doctor gave the good news she could go home, but he needed to speak with them before leaving the next day.

"What does he want?"

"I'm not sure, but I imagine it's about my test results."

Pete paced. "Why? You're fine! I hope this doesn't take too long. I've missed enough work already!"

"I'm exhausted, Pete, and I'd like to get some rest. Why don't you go on home? I'll see you in the morning." Mary Ann showed a brave face.

Pete left the room without saying goodbye or a departing kiss.

The next morning, he returned and found Mary Ann already dressed, waiting for him. They approached the doctor's office and took their seats by his desk.

"Okay, Doc, why are we here?" Pete blurted out, the tone of his voice anxious. "Can you make this short and sweet? I need to get back to work."

Mary Ann reached over and put her hand on Pete's arm. "Calm down. Give the doctor a chance to talk."

"Mr. and Mrs. Tobias, I'm sorry, but I'm afraid the news isn't good. The results from the tests indicate you have stage four cancer, which has metastasized throughout your body. I'm afraid it is inoperable."

"That's ridiculous; it can't be. She's been fine up until two days ago!"

"No. I haven't been fine. For some time now, I haven't felt well."

"Why didn't you say something? So, you've felt sick but didn't say anything and didn't go to see the doctor? What *were* you thinking?"

"For that very reason, Pete. I didn't want you to get all upset."

Pete stood and shouted, "Upset? *Upset*! This is a little more than *upset*; the doctor told us you have inoperable cancer, and I'm supposed to remain calm? And *you're* supposed to take this news without question?"

She turned to the doctor calmly and asked, "Is there anything we can do, Doctor?"

"I'm afraid not, Mrs. Tobias. The cancer is Ewing Sarcoma, an aggressive type of bone cancer, and there isn't anything we can do except try to make you as comfortable as possible."

"How much time do I have, Doctor?"

"Your condition will worsen. I'm afraid you'll have possibly two months, three at the most. I'm sorry." The doctor lowered his eyes.

BAD NEWS

"You're *sorry?* According to you, my wife has two, possibly three months to live, and you're *sorry?* We're going to get a second opinion!"

"No, we aren't. We're going to deal with this and make the best of the situation. I've suspected something was wrong for some time. I had no idea it was this bad, though. We will deal with it. The doctors ran all the tests—I trust their prognosis. I'm too exhausted to go through more tests. Let me spend what time I have left relishing each day and enjoying every second of it." She turned to the doctor and said, "Thank you, Doctor."

"But Mary Ann!"

"Pete, let's go—*now!*"

On the trip home, they spoke very little. Pete's knuckles were white as he gripped the steering wheel while Mary Ann sat quietly next to him with her hand gently resting on his knee. Pete pulled in front of their house, and before she got out of the car, Mary Ann broke the silence.

"Pete, I don't want Jonathan to know anything is wrong. Until it becomes too obvious to keep it a secret any longer, promise me you won't tell him."

"There you go again, protecting *his* precious feelings. He should know his mother is dying!"

"Why? Would that change anything? I don't want this to distract our lives. And I think I've already been preparing myself for the worst—you don't know how long I've been dealing with weakness, feeling ill, and not feeling like myself."

"You don't want this to be a distraction in our lives? How can it *not* be a distraction? *You're dying!* I still don't understand why you didn't share this with me. I'm your *husband*; we vowed for better or worse, in sickness and health, till death do us part. Why did you leave me out?"

"It wasn't because I don't love you. I know how easily you get upset, and I simply couldn't deal with your anger and frustration. Today, for example: in the doctor's office, it was difficult for the doctor—I could tell—and you weren't making it any easier. Let's try to live as normally as we can for the time I have left. *Please!* Can you do this for me?"

She pleaded, fighting back the tears. Mary Ann got out of the car, leaned in the open car window, and locked eyes with Pete. "Please, can you just do this one thing for me?"

"Sure, whatever you want! I have to get back to work." He sped off, leaving her on the sidewalk with tears in her eyes.

FIVE

END IS NEAR

Over the next few weeks, Jonathan noticed his father hadn't raised his voice very much, and he was more attentive to Mom, helping her with the dishes after dinner. Jonathan couldn't remember him *ever* doing that. Mom seemed to need to sit down and rest more often. She hadn't needed that much rest before her fainting spell. The atmosphere around the house was less tense too. He couldn't put his finger on it, but it seemed like his father was kinder and more understanding than Jonathan could ever remember, particularly to Mom. It felt like something had drastically changed since the hospital, but they kept whatever it was to themselves. He felt excluded, which felt strange and awkward since his mother shared almost everything with him.

He made a point of being conscientious and prompt about getting home on time since the blow-up with his father. Since his mother's strange fainting attack, he did everything he could to smooth things over. But he spent most of his time worried about his mom; she hadn't been at all the same since returning from her first visit to the hospital. Jonathan wanted to talk about it but feared the worst, so he was afraid to force the conversation. It was a stressful time for him, always worried and scared. His parents attempted to carry on as if nothing was wrong when it was evident something was wrong—*terribly wrong.*

He finally decided to say something to her. "Mom, something isn't right, and I need to know what's going on with you. Are you sick? Please don't keep me in the dark about this. I'm worried about you!"

"I'm fine, son. The doctor said I am a little anemic; that's why I've been so tired lately."

"Are you sure? You and dad have been acting strange."

"What do you mean *strange*?"

"Dad has been super nice." He smiled at the irony of his words and looked at her quizzically. "And the two of you are talking more than you used to. What's going on? I feel like there is some secret the two of you are keeping from me."

"I think it's your imagination, Jonathan. Your father was worried after I had to go to the hospital. That's all."

"Okay, if you are sure."

"I'm sure, son."

Mary Ann grabbed a book off the end table and laid down on the couch. Jonathan headed to the basement door but looked back at her increasingly frail figure and felt sad. He grabbed his phone and called Mark to ask to meet at the café. Jonathan wanted to share his concerns and talk things through. When Mark agreed to meet, Jonathan pecked his mom's cheek softly so as not to wake her, and headed out.

The atmosphere in the café helped Jonathan breathe a little easier. When Mark walked in, he waved him over. "Thanks for meeting me. Listen, I am worried about my mom. I think she's really sick. It started with her fainting attack and hospital stay. She's been exhausted ever since then, doesn't look right, and my dad isn't acting like normal."

"What do you mean?"

"Well, he's being *nice* and not screaming all the time. I feel like something is going on with Mom, but neither of my parents will tell me anything. They try to act as if nothing is wrong."

END IS NEAR

"Well, maybe nothing's wrong, and it's only your imagination. She's probably okay, and your dad is trying to make up for the way he carried on that night. You said he really upset her by yelling at you."

"No, my father isn't like that. He's being nice because he's worried about her. I don't understand why they aren't saying anything to me, though."

"You know, you could *just ask*?"

"I did *just ask* my mom. She said she is anemic; that's why she's so tired all of the time, but I don't believe her. It's more than that." Jonathan shook his head.

Without reaching any solution but grateful for Mark's friendship, they left the café and went their separate ways, but Jonathan continued to worry about his mom.

In his room later that night, Jonathan grabbed his journal and wrote.

> *I know there is something terribly wrong with mom. The other day, she practically fainted when she reached down to pick up the kitchen towel she had dropped. I rushed over to help her, but she assured me she just had a headrush from standing up too fast. But she looked pale and seemed to move slower than usual that day. But truthfully, I don't think I've seen her move at her normal speed since. I don't get it because neither she nor dad wants to tell me about it. Why are they excluding me? I deserve to know what's going on. I feel like they are treating me like I'm still a kid or something. Why?*

∞

In the passing days, Mary Ann's condition deteriorated rapidly. She had another seizure that required another trip to the hospital. It was clear to Jonathan his mother was seriously unwell, and he pressed his father for information while in the hospital waiting room.

"Dad, what's going on with mom? I want to know. *I'm scared.*"

"Your mother is seriously ill."

"I got that; she's back in the hospital a second time—here we are again, so what's wrong with her? I want to know. I *need* to know."

"She didn't want to worry you—she has cancer. Your mom has always protected you like you're still a child," Pete blurted it out without showing any affection.

"Holy cow! What? How bad is it?"

"I'm afraid she won't be with us much longer. The doctors gave her three months originally, but it has progressed much faster than they expected."

Jonathan collapsed in a nearby chair and sobbed uncontrollably. "Oh, God, how can this be happening? It's not fair; it's not right, not mom!"

Pete just looked down at him. "Men don't bawl like some baby. Listen, I'm going to go in and be with your mother. When you pull yourself together, you better get in there also." Pete walked back into Mary Ann's hospital room.

"I'll be right in." Jonathan wiped at his tears.

Shortly after, Jonathan joined them. He saw his mother hooked up to machines making weird beeping sounds. She was pale, her complexion looked gray, the dark circles under her eyes were more pronounced, and her body seemed frail and helpless. The woman lying there changed to a mere shadow of the woman he knew as his mother. She was conscious and gave him a faint smile as he entered the room. Pete sat at her bedside. Jonathan went to the other side and took his mother's hand; she smiled her always comforting smile. She could tell he had been crying by his red puffy eyes.

"I am so sorry you're sick. I wish I could do something."

"I'm afraid there isn't anything you or anyone can do, my dear. I love you so very much. Listen, the two of you, there is something you two need to do for me."

"What is it, Mom?"

She took both their hands in hers. "Promise me you will take care of each other; promise me you will do this for me. I need to know that *both* of the men in my life will be okay when I'm gone."

"Yes, Mom, I will."

"Sure, hun, I love you."

She smiled at them and closed her eyes. They sat in silence, looking at the look of peace on Mary Ann's now-sleeping face. Suddenly, the beeping machines stopped, and a single dull tone sounded. Jonathan screamed for help, and a nurse rushed into the room. Though she checked Mary Ann and frowned at the lack of a pulse, she didn't act surprised.

"I'm very sorry," she said. "Mary Ann wanted to go peacefully, and it appears she went while surrounded by the two loves of her life." The nurse turned off her machines and asked them to take a few minutes to say goodbye as she stepped out of the room, pulling both the curtain and door behind her.

Jonathan began to cry, still grasping his mother's hand. "Mom! Oh, Mom! No!" He sobbed in silence for a few minutes.

Pete bent over and gently kissed her lips and said, "Goodbye, my love." Then, he turned to Jonathan. "C'mon, there isn't anything more we can do here."

"I'll be there in a minute. I want to sit with her for a few more minutes."

"Well, I'm leaving, and if you don't want to have to walk home, you'll leave when I do."

"Go on without me. I'll be fine."

Jonathan sat there for a while, but eventually, he made his way home. When he arrived, the house was empty and dark like the light that had made it *home* had gone out forever. He went to his room and wrote what was going through his mind.

I think this was the most horrible day of my life. I can't believe I will never see her standing at the kitchen stove with a smile on her face or hear her warm hello. What will it be like never getting to hug her again? Oh, Mom, what's it going to be like around here without you? What's it going to be like living with Dad? I wonder where he is? We have to make arrangements for your funeral. Dad and I need to talk. Why would he disappear at a time like this? I can't do this on my own! He's probably down at the bar . . .

Then, he started to cry.

The next few days were some of the darkest in Jonathan's life. His mother's loss was a devastating blow for him; his friends consoled him as best they could, but it didn't help.
"I don't know what to do about Jon," Kate said.
"What do you mean?"
"Well, he is so depressed and seems so helpless."
"Listen, all we can do is be there for him. The poor guy watched the most important person in his life die a painful, lingering death. You have to expect him to be a mess right now. We need to give him some space. You don't need to be Florence Nightingale to the rescue!"
"I hate seeing him in so much pain," Kate said.
"I do, too, but there isn't anything we can do or say right now that's going to make this any easier on him," Mark offered.

Mary Ann's funeral was beautiful. Kate's father, Reverend Kenneth Hogan, officiated at the service and graveside.

Jonathan needed to have his friends and their parents with him. He hadn't seen Mark or Kate's parents in some time; it brought back good memories of when the three were children, and Jonathan felt happy.

During her funeral and the celebration of Mary Ann's life, many of his mother's friends consoled him. They shared anecdotes and remembered their encounters with her. Mrs. Davis told him how she had helped her through a difficult time when her daughter ran away. When Mrs. Marcus' family from across the street lost their heat during the winter, Mary Ann let them stay at their home for the few hours it took to replace their furnace. It was a beautiful story about how the two prepared dinner for both families and turned a bad situation into a party with fun and laughter. Everyone spoke of her kind and gentle heart and generous nature and their fond memories of her.

Mr. and Mrs. Atkins approached Jonathan. She hugged him, and he shook Jonathan's hand. "Listen, if there is anything we can do, please let us know."

"Thanks so much. I appreciate it. Things are difficult for me right now, but I'll be okay, and thank Mark for me also."

"You know he is always there if you need him, Jonathan."

After the funeral and the celebration of Mary Ann's life, Jonathan and Pete headed home but didn't speak on the drive back. When Jonathan got into the house, he dropped into a chair and sobbed.

Pete came in shortly, closed the door, and went over to Jonathan. Without warning, he shouted in Jonathan's face, "I want you out of here as soon as possible! You've mooched off of me for twenty-three years. But now, your mother isn't here to protect you anymore. I want you gone. Do you hear me—*gone*! If your stuff isn't out of here by the time I return from work tomorrow, you'll find it on the sidewalk, and I am changing the locks."

"But I thought we were going to look after each other like Mom wanted?"

"Your mother is *gone*. I've looked after you for far too long, and I want you out of my house *tomorrow*. You're lazy, a good for nothing, and I want you out of my life!" Abruptly, Pete stormed out of the house, slammed the door, got in the car, and drove off, squealing the tires on the pavement.

Jonathan sat there, astonished. He buried his face in his hands, shocked, frightened, and dismayed, not wholly comprehending what just happened. He had just buried his mother and had no place to live. So, he stood up, looked around in confusion at what his life had become, and decided to go out. Locking the door behind him, he left the house and walked the short distance to the cemetery to his mother's grave.

He squatted at his mom's resting place and talked to her, sensing her with him. "Hi, Mom. I wanted to tell you the funeral was beautiful. So many people had wonderful things to say. I'm not the only person who misses you. Lots of people loved you, and you touched a lot of lives. But I don't know what I will do right now. I miss you so much, and Dad kicked me out of the house. So, I feel lost. He cried softly. The tears moistened the fresh dirt under his feet.

SIX

AFTERMATH AND DEBATE

A short time later, Jonathan returned to the house. He stood in his room and looked around at what had been his world for twenty-three years. As he began throwing his possessions in a box, he saw his journal and sat down for a few minutes to write.

Dear Mom,

I love and miss you so much already. Dad lied to you on your deathbed. He had no intention of honoring your last wish about us taking care of each other after you were gone. You didn't deserve the way he treated you. I know he's hated me since the day I was born and blamed you. I'm sorry that I caused your life to be so miserable with him. Please forgive me.

Your Loving Son,
Jonathan

Then, he called Mark. "Hey, buddy, can I ask you for a favor?"

Mark sensed the desperation as Jonathan's voice cracked with emotion. "What's going on? What happened?"

"My father just kicked me out of the house, and I have to find someplace by tomorrow."

"What?"

"My father disowned me! He kicked me out!"

"What? I don't believe this! You just buried your mother, and he already kicked you out?"

"Yes! He said he's taken care of me for long enough. Now that mom is gone, he wants me out of his house." His voice shook with despair, and his eyes glistened with tears and puffed red from crying.

"Unbelievable! I knew you guys didn't get along, but I never thought he would do something like this."

"Well, he has! I should have expected it; he has always hated me. So, can I crash on your couch for a couple of days until I figure out what I'm going to do?"

"Yeah, sure. Do you want me to come over to your place to help you get your stuff out of there? Where's your father now?"

"I don't know. He told me to get out by tomorrow. Then, he got in the car and peeled out of here. I don't know where he went, and honestly, I don't care anymore. Yes, please help me pack up and get out of here if you can."

"Sure. I'll be there soon. Hang in there, buddy," Mark said.

After they hung up, Jonathan glanced at his space in the basement and sighed. Where would he begin? Wiping his eyes dry, Jonathan began to pack his belongings. Though he needed time to absorb all his sorrow, he felt pressured to keep moving. He feared the repercussions if he wasn't out promptly.

Before he knew it, thirty minutes had passed. A knock on the front door jerked him out of his concentration. Then, Mark called out.

"Hey, Jon, where are you?"

"I'm downstairs in my room."

AFTERMATH AND DEBATE

Jonathan heard footsteps coming downstairs. He turned to greet Mark but saw Kate with him.

"Kate, what are you doing here?"

"Well, that's a dumb question. Do you think I am going to sit at home after what Mark told me happened? My parents are in total shock!"

"I didn't figure Mark would call you. You told your parents?"

"Well, yeah, of course, I told my parents! What your father did sucks!"

"I thought you would want her to know, buddy. And I told my parents too."

"Geez! Everyone knows now! Oh, what difference does it make?" He waved his hand to shun away the thought. "Let's get my stuff out of here as fast as we can. I don't care if I ever see his face again!" Kate frowned as Mark tapped Jonathan's shoulder, offering him comfort. Then, the friends packed the contents of Jonathan's room into whatever they could find—an old suitcase, grocery bags, boxes—and after several trips up and down the stairs, they loaded everything into Mark's car and Kate's father's van. As he left his home for the last time, Jonathan locked the front door and pushed the keys through the mail slot. He turned back and looked at the house one last time. With an aching heart, he headed off to Mark's. Now that his mother was gone, the house had lost its soul and meant nothing to him anymore. As he took one last glance in the rearview mirror as he rode away, he saw it for what it would have been without his mom—a hellhole.

∞

Later that evening, after Jonathan and Mark stopped to eat and picked up a six-pack of beer, they settled in at Mark's apartment. Jonathan's meager belongings sat here and there, scattered around the living room in the small apartment.

"I can't thank you enough, buddy, for letting me crash on your couch for a couple of days until I get my life sorted out."

"Not a problem! What are friends for but to help in a jam? And Kate feels the same way."

As they sat and drank a beer each, the severity of Jonathan's situation sank in as he contemplated what to do next.

He blurted out, "What am I going to do now?"

"Well, you've complained about living with your father for years. Now you've got what you wanted; it's probably for the best anyway."

"What do you mean by *that*?"

"Well, your father has treated you like crap your whole life; it's probably best you're away from him and out on your own. That's all I'm saying."

"You're probably right. I guess I thought it would be on *my* terms and not like this—the *same day as mom's funeral*. I can't believe him! On her death bed, she asked us to take care of each other. He lied and said yes. What a miserable, two-faced, lying jerk! All he's ever cared about was himself! Ugh! I hate him!" Jonathan punched the pillow and looked off to hide his tears. They sat in silence as Mark felt just being there may give Jonathan some comfort. He flipped the TV on to offer distraction, and they had another couple of beers and decided to talk more about it after work the next day. Soon, Jonathan passed out on the couch.

The following morning, Jonathan returned to work as if nothing had happened. Mr. Jacobs came into the mailroom and asked, "What are you doing here, Jonathan? Your mother just passed away; you can take a couple of days off."

"Thanks, Mr. Jacobs, but I need to keep busy."

"Okay, but if you need time, please let me know."

AFTERMATH AND DEBATE

Geez! Maybe the old man has a heart after all.

Jonathan focused on work all day to keep his mind off his troubles. Mr. Jacobs' compassion threw Jonathan off, and he appreciated that softer side of him.

The day passed quickly. That evening, Jonathan returned to Mark's apartment after work and found Mark looking at a document.

"Hey, what do you have there, buddy?"

"It's something Kate talked to me about several weeks ago, and we've been thinking about telling you about it since your mom passed away."

He handed Jonathan the paper.

Jonathan read the document, and with a shocked look on his face, he exclaimed, "Are you out of your mind? You can't be seriously considering this!"

Mark asked, "Why not? I've been thinking about it for weeks now. I thought we could all go but figured you had too much going on in your life before. But now you don't."

"You are going on an archaeological dig to *Israel* to research some old *Biblical king*? Am I reading this correctly?"

Nodding with a smile, Mark replied, "King Solomon, to be specific."

"Why would you want to do something like this? What makes you think *I* would want to do something like this?"

"Kate's dad is a Biblical scholar and particularly interested in Solomon. Solomon was said to be the wisest king in Biblical history. He's a bit of a mystery. No one knows a lot about him except for the few references we have from the Bible."

"I might have heard that name mentioned when I was a kid; we didn't do much with the Bible at home. You *are* kidding me about doing this, aren't you?"

"Why not? Neither of us has anything to keep us here, and it is only for two months."

"What about all the big *important lawyer* stuff you do?"

"I've already asked if I can take a leave of absence, and they said I could. Mr. Simmons, the head of the firm, is very supportive and realizes what an opportunity this is to do something I would probably never experience otherwise. He's a great guy and understands this trip could help make me a better person *and* a better employee. Besides, he said they could manage for two months without me."

"What about your parents?"

"Duh. I've already spoken to my parents, and they think it would be a good thing for me to do. It's a chance to learn something about myself. And besides, I'm an adult. I don't have to ask for my parent's permission. And you don't have to ask your father either."

"Well, I already know what they will say at the mill. They'll fire me for sure. But I guess that doesn't matter anymore. I hate that job anyway and only took it because my father got it for me. In his mind, he thought I would work my way up the ladder there. He thought if I worked in the office, I'd *have more opportunities to be someone better than a blue-collar worker like him.* Hmph." Jonathan imitated his father and rolled his eyes. "Fat chance it'd ever happen in *that* place."

"Hey, what did you say this king's name was again?"

"King Solomon."

"Hm. Wait, I guess I remember a little about him now. Wasn't he the wise *and fabulously rich* king?"

"Yeah, I suppose that's true, but that isn't why we are going; this isn't some *treasure hunt*. Kate's dad is also an amateur archeologist in charge of the dig. This is something he's wanted to do for some time now. Since he was a kid, King Solomon has fascinated him. So, through his Biblical research, he recently received grant money. And the Israel Ministry of Foreign Affairs and the Israel Antiquities Authority granted permission for the dig. He's looking for volunteers to help," Mark explained.

"So, Kate's father is heading this archaeology thing up? And you said Kate is going too?"

"Well, yeah, as I said, her father is organizing the whole thing. Do you think Kate would miss a chance like this?"

"You're right. Doing something crazy like this would be right up Kate's alley. But I don't have any archaeological experience. I don't have much experience *at all*." Jonathan's voice trailed off.

"Well, neither do Kate or me; that's the beauty of it. We don't need any experience. We'll be doing grunt work like digging, hauling buckets of earth, cleaning pottery sherds, categorizing, and documenting stuff. Maybe we'll learn something too."

"How much is this going to cost? As you know, I only have several hundred saved up."

"Well, we'll have to get some gear, but grant money is funding the trip."

"I don't know." Jonathan shook his head.

"Excuses, *excuses*! Listen, this archeological dig isn't going to be a *vacation*, but it could be an adventure!"

"An *adventure*?"

Jonathan continued to protest. "I've never been more than one hundred miles from Harrington in my whole life."

"What? You've got to be kidding me, *never*?"

"Nope."

"That's unbelievable. After all these years of being friends, I never knew that about you. Have you been living under a rock?"

"I don't think my father has even been that far out of town in his whole life. He always said everything he needed was right here in Harrington, so he didn't need to go anywhere else."

"Unbelievable!"

Jonathan paced around the room. He said, "And besides, don't you need a passport to leave the country? I don't have a passport, so I can't possibly go."

Mark countered, "Buddy, that's just another *excuse*! We still need them too. Come on, now is the perfect time to do something like this. As I said before, we don't have anything important enough to keep us from taking this opportunity."

Their back-and-forth discussion continued for some time as Jonathan asked questions, and Mark tried to persuade his friend to come along. In the end, Mark told Jonathan the adventure was a once-in-a-lifetime chance to do something special. With that comment, Jonathan's ears perked up—*do something special!*

Mark continued, "Besides, you like puzzles and figuring out how things work. This could be a real-life puzzle discovering clues and uncovering mysteries from the past."

But all Jonathan heard was the part about doing something special—being someone special—*someone famous!*

Later that night, after Mark had gone to bed, Jonathan lounged on the couch, mulling all this over in his head. As usual, he found writing helped him clarify his thoughts. He pulled out his journal from his backpack and began to write.

I can't believe Mark and Kate are seriously considering going on this archaeological expedition. Why would they want to go halfway around the globe to dig in the dirt for two months? Why would they think I wanted to go? So much has happened to me already—this job at the mill, Mom's death, Dad kicked me out—and now my two best friends—my only friends—want me to go traipsing off with them on some crazy adventure.

On the other hand, Mark did say it was a once-in-a-lifetime chance to do something special. What if I found the old king's treasure? I would be famous! Then, Dad would be proud of me. I would be rich! There must be some kind of finder's fee for finding a treasure? It couldn't be all that bad. I'd be getting away from here for a couple of months. It might give me a chance to figure out what I will do now that my world has fallen apart. Maybe it's not such a crazy idea after all? Besides, I'd be with Mark and Kate.

SEVEN

DECISIONS, PLANS, AND PREPARATIONS

Jonathan hardly slept that night. He considered the *security* of staying in Harrington—which is all he ever knew—and continued to live his miserable, boring life there. Or could he take a chance to find out what was outside the comfort of Harrington, in the world, and possibly become someone special? *Besides, Mark said this is a once-in-a-lifetime experience. Why should they have all the fun? I need to get away from this town anyway.* The thoughts fluttered around in his mind as he finally drifted off to sleep.

The next morning before he left for work, Jonathan made up his mind and committed to going on the dig with his friends.

"Hey, that's great, man! I'll let Kate know, and I'll go ask her dad."

"Wait a minute! You mean to tell me you sprung all this on me last night, and you haven't even confirmed with her dad that we can go?"

"Well, no, I wanted to make sure you were in before I asked him."

"Seriously? Talk about *unbelievable!*" Jonathan headed out for work in a huff. He got himself psyched up to be *someone special* but didn't even have permission to go on the journey.

∞

After work, Mark stopped by Kate's house and talked with her father about Jonathan and the dig. Kate joined in the conversation, excited about the possibility, but her dad wondered if the trip was right for Jonathan.

"I have total confidence that you'll be fine, but I have some concerns about Jonathan."

"I'm sure he'll be okay, Reverend Hogan."

"Well, I'm not so sure. This trip is a *major* undertaking. The conditions can be brutal, but it is vital to my research. I need to be sure everyone will pitch in, follow directions, and do their jobs. Jonathan has been through a lot lately. I don't know if his head is in the right place for a trip like this."

"I understand, sir."

"I'm certain you do—and thank you. Why don't you bring him around tomorrow night for dinner, and we'll all sit down and talk about it?"

"Thank you, sir. We'll be there."

He thanked him for his time, said bye to Kate, and walked down the sidewalk, lost in his thoughts. *Hopefully, Kate and I are right about bringing Jon along on this trip. I am crossing my fingers. We'll see at dinner tomorrow night how it goes when we can discuss things in more detail.*

When Mark returned to the apartment, Jonathan was waiting for him. "Well, what did Reverend Hogan say?"

"He and Mrs. Hogan invited us over for dinner tomorrow to talk about the trip."

"Well, does that mean yes?"

DECISIONS, PLANS, AND PREPARATIONS

"I think it means he wants to talk with us about the trip and explain what he expects and what needs to happen."

"It's me, isn't it?"

"What do you mean by that?"

"He figures I am going to screw something up, doesn't he? I'm certain he's aware of all the troubles I've had in the past. After all, he *has* known us since we were kids."

"Uh, I think he only wants to make sure the three of us know his expectations. I've already told you—this isn't going to be a vacation; it's going to be hard work—plenty of it—and in the desert heat. Reverend Hogan wants to make sure we're all up for it. He has already talked to the other dig team members and wants to bring us up to speed."

"It's me; I know it! *The screwup*!"

"Oh, will you *stop*!"

"Okay, so, I shouldn't be concerned Kate's dad might think I'm not good enough to go?"

"I think you doubt yourself and your capabilities. It's time you start changing your attitude. You aren't living under your father's thumb anymore. It's time for you to man-up! You're as good as the next person and *as capable, but* you need to start believing that about yourself. What better way to find out who you are and what you're capable of if not on a trip like this."

He put his hand up. "Okay, okay; I got it."

Later, he wrote in his journal.

I know it's me. I just know it's me! Reverend Hogan thinks I will screw something up, or I'm not good enough to go on his stupid expedition. He doesn't doubt Mark or Kate, but me, well, that's a different story. That's why he wants to have us over for dinner so he can check me out and decide if I am good enough. What's wrong with me that no one can trust me to do anything right? I know I've had a tough time of it in the past, but I've never gotten a break. Everyone thinks I'm nothing but a screwup. It's not my fault! It's not my fault! What's it gonna take for me to get a break? I thought this was it, but even Reverend Hogan doesn't have faith that I can do it. I know it's me—he has a problem with me!

∞

The next evening, Mark and Jonathan showed up at the Hogans' at 6:00 p.m. for dinner. Kate greeted them at the door with a big hug.

"How are you guys tonight?" she asked.

"Doin' good," Mark replied.

"Fine, thanks. How about you?"

"Just a little hectic getting ready for finals and the end of the term. C'mon in."

Reverend and Mrs. Hogan greeted them with a handshake and a hug. Jonathan had forgotten what a lovely couple they were. He was tall and handsome, slightly graying at the temples, and Mrs. Hogan was elegant with that same beautiful, auburn hair Kate inherited.

She said, "It's lovely to see you boys, or should I say, *young men*. It's hard for me to imagine you all grown up. By the way, I'm so sorry for your loss, Jonathan."

Jonathan nodded.

Mark added excitedly, "Thanks, Mrs. Hogan. It's nice of you to have us over for dinner."

"Thanks, Reverend Hogan, for your kind words at my mom's funeral. It meant a lot to me to have you all there and Mark's parents too."

He placed his hand on Jonathan's shoulder, "I was honored to perform the service, Jonathan. Your mother was a wonderful woman. How's your father doing?"

"I wouldn't know, sir. I haven't seen or spoken to him since Mom's funeral."

"Oh, I didn't realize that."

DECISIONS, PLANS, AND PREPARATIONS

Kate interjected. "What do you mean, Dad? I told you Jon's father kicked him out of the house right after they got home from the funeral."

With an embarrassed glance, Mrs. Hogan took her husband's arm. "Well, enough about that. Dinner is almost ready, so let's go in and sit down."

At the table, Jonathan, Mark, and Kate chattered back and forth like they did when they were kids having dinner at the Hogans'. The evening brought back such great memories for Jonathan.

While around the dinner table, Reverend Hogan discussed tidbits about the trip, and everyone paid close attention.

"I want you all to understand this archaeological dig is significant to the research I have been conducting, and it is serious business, *not a vacation*. We are going to be excavating at a site, and previous workers have already partially uncovered some artifacts, which has led to the presumption that this is one of the palaces King Solomon inhabited outside Jerusalem. To this date, there is no clear evidence of any connection. So, we're going to attempt to clarify that on this expedition. Is that clear to all three of you? I know you three have known each other your whole lives, and I don't want that familiarity to interfere with our job on the dig. Do you all understand?"

Jonathan, Mark, and Kate all replied in unison, "Understood!"

"Further, there will be harsh conditions you are not accustomed to here, so we are all going to have to adapt and not let that hamper what we are there to achieve."

All the time he talked, Reverend Hogan watched Jonathan out of the corner of his eye, wanting to see his reaction. But Jonathan didn't flinch and listened with interest and attention. "Are there any questions?"

Jonathan asked, "Sir, I don't have a passport. Is there time for me to get one?"

"All three of you need passports, and some of the other team members do, too, so I am making arrangements for all the documents we will need. But you will still need to fill out your paperwork and take passport photos, get certified copies of your birth certificates, immunizations, and other additional documentation to verify your identities." Reverend Hogan stood up, went to another room, and returned with two manila folders. One had Jonathan's name on it, and the other had Mark's name. "Here are all the documents you will need to fill out for your travel documents, passports, and the list of the equipment you will need to purchase for the trip. Things will need time to process, so please make sure you get your paperwork filled out immediately, and then get everything on that list."

Jonathan and Mark took their folders. They exchanged some additional conversation and pleasantries, then said their thanks and left.

As they left, Reverend Hogan said to them, "I've known you fellas your whole lives. After all that time, you can drop the formalities, and please call me Reverend Ken."

Mark and Jonathan thanked him for a lovely evening and said, "We'll talk soon."

As they departed down the sidewalk, Reverend Hogan told Kate and his wife he was still worried Jonathan wasn't up to the task.

Kate countered, "Listen, Dad. Jon has had a rough time his whole life. You know how his father is and how he's treated Jon. Give him a chance to maybe, *just maybe*, change his life around. He needs someone to have confidence in him, someone who cares and has faith in him."

As a smile crossed his face, he said, "I think he already has someone who cares about him, young lady."

"Oh, Dad!" She playfully jabbed her father and hurried off so he wouldn't see her blush. She felt her old feelings for Jonathan pop to the surface again.

DECISIONS, PLANS, AND PREPARATIONS

Mrs. Hogan looked from her daughter to her husband, questioningly. But she didn't say anything, only shrugged her shoulders. She disappeared into the kitchen to finish clearing the dinner dishes, and Reverend Hogan went into his study to prepare for the trip.

Once Mark and Jonathan returned to the apartment, Jonathan said, "Well, do you think he will let me come on the dig?"

"He gave you the folder with your name on it, so I guess that's a pretty good indication that you're going."

"Wow. So, after hearing him talk about the dig, I truly want to do this now. And I can see how important it is to him for the trip to be successful."

"I told you this was his life's work, and he is counting on the whole dig team to be there for him."

"Yeah, it must be great to have such passion for something. It gave me chills just listening to Reverend Ken."

Mark added, "Reverend Ken can get pretty passionate when he talks about archaeology. On this expedition, we'll be doing something special."

There it was again, doing something special! Jonathan thought.

That night, they made plans to get everything ready. They had three weeks before departing for Israel. Mark reminded him they'd both need to continue to work until it was time to leave. The extra money in those few weeks would be helpful.

"I'll need to give a two-week notice," Jonathan remembered.

"Why? Are you planning to go back to work there when we return? You said they are going to fire you anyway when you tell them about the trip."

"I know, but it's the right thing to do. Especially after Mr. Jacobs showed me compassion after my mom died. Don't you have to give the law firm your notice?"

"Nah. Remember I told you I already talked to my boss about going on the trip. He gave me permission to go weeks ago. But I'll need to tell them when."

Jonathan nodded and considered how nice it must be to have an understanding boss, something he felt he never had.

∞

The three weeks passed very quickly as they purchased their equipment, including sturdy shoes and leather gloves. Jonathan read about Jerusalem and learned it was over five thousand years old. He also found Bible references about King Solomon and recent information on the palace they'd excavate on the dig. They also had two meetings with Reverend Ken and the other members of the U.S. dig team.

Mark made the arrangements to take a leave of absence from the law firm. The day Jonathan told Mr. Jacobs about the trip, he was copying documents in the mailroom.

"Mr. Jacobs, can I speak with you for a minute?"

"What is it, Jonathan? Can't you see I am busy here doing something *you* are supposed to be doing? Where have you been?"

"That's what I want to talk to you about, sir."

Well, what is it?"

"I'd like to give you my notice. Recently, I received an opportunity to participate in an archaeological expedition with Reverend Hogan to Israel."

"You're what?" Mr. Jacobs appeared genuinely shocked.

"Sir, I'm giving my notice."

"You're giving up a good, secure job here at the mill to galavant on some expedition with *Ken Hogan?*"

"Yes, sir, my friends are also going. It's an important expedition for Reverend Hogan, and I am excited to be part of it."

"What's your father think about this? He went to a lot of trouble to get you this job."

That's it. I tried to be nice. I'm tired of hearing that! "If I hear one more person tell me my father went to a lot of trouble to

DECISIONS, PLANS, AND PREPARATIONS

get me this job, I'm going to scream! I don't care, Mr. Jacobs! *I don't care!* And if what I read in those documents—the ones you had me pass out a couple of months ago—comes true, you all may be looking for *secure jobs!*" Jonathan used air quotes and smiled.

"What do you mean?"

"That's right; if things don't turn around here in a big way real soon, this place is going under, and you'll all be looking for jobs! Bye, Mr. Jacobs, and good luck!"

As he left the building, Jonathan loved the shocked look on Jacobs' face, "Man, that felt so good. Maybe *he* doesn't even know what's coming."

That night, Jonathan and Mark finished checking out their equipment in preparation for the trip. Mark said good night and went off to bed. Jonathan wasn't tired yet, so he took out his journal and wrote a few lines.

Am I doing the right thing? What made me think I could do this? I've never gone anywhere or been good at anything, except maybe video games. I want to go and be a part of this, but at the same time, I am terrified! What's wrong with me? Mark says I need to man up, get out of my comfort zone, and be a part of something special. Will this be the break I've been hoping for in my life or just another failure? I want to be someone special. I need to do something special. You're nobody unless you achieve something special. Mark and Kate have it all, great futures, wonderful parents. What do I have? I'm homeless and now without a job or anything to look forward to—a loser.

Jonathan had a fitful night's sleep filled with excitement and apprehension and what it possibly held for his future.

The morning of their departure, Jonathan and Mark met the vans to take them to the airport. Everyone was there; parents said goodbye to their kids, and Mark and Jonathan met up with the other members of the dig team. The air was charged with excitement and anticipation. Jonathan felt it in the pit of his stomach as everyone loaded their gear in the vans. They said last-minute goodbyes as everyone boarded the vans, buckled in, and departed for the airport.

Jonathan looked out the van window as they left town with a queasy, excited feeling in the pit of his stomach. *Well, there's no turning back now! Will you return to this town still a loser? Or will this trip change your life forever?*

EIGHT

STRANGER IN A STRANGE LAND

After the fifty-mile commute over two-lane roads, the dig team arrived at the airport. They deposited their baggage and headed to clear security. When Jonathan handed his documents to the TSA officer, he mistakenly gave him his social security card instead of his driver's license. Mark and Kate had a good laugh at that, but Jonathan didn't think it was that funny. They had a brief wait before boarding their plane, which Jonathan used to nervously pace in the terminal waiting area.

"Why don't you come and sit down next to me and relax?" Kate suggested.

He tried to keep his panic under control by pacing, but internally, he was trying to keep his breathing steady. "I never thought I would be so frightened to get on an airplane!"

"Don't worry. The three of us will sit together on the plane. Try to be calm. Everything is going to be fine." Kate stood up and walked over to Jonathan and put her hand on his arm to reassure him. With her other hand, she gripped his hand gently and squeezed it as she gave him a comforting smile.

"I know, but you need to convince my stomach of that. I hope I don't throw up!" He put his hand on his stomach, trying to quell his nausea.

"Calm down," Mark said with an eye roll. "Here are a couple Dramamine™ for air sickness. Take these; you'll be fine, buddy. We're going to be right there with you all of the way."

Jonathan followed them onto the plane. He struggled to take his seat and had not realized until this moment that he was claustrophobic. Jonathan nervously awaited takeoff as he leaned back into his seat and said, "This will be easy. This will be easy. This will be easy."

As the plane took off, Jonathan closed his eyes and gripped the armrest as tight as a vice grip. He felt Kate's hand grab his and instantly felt secure, knowing he wasn't alone. As the plane reached altitude, he cautiously opened his eyes and took in the wonder of the view out his window. The clouds beneath him took his breath away. The sun was so bright; it made the large, billowing cumulus clouds blindingly white as the plane flew through them, and the sky was an incredible shade of blue.

The expression on Jonathan's face was priceless as he turned to face Kate and Mark in the seats next to him. "Wow. This is so beautiful! It seems surreal to think we are in the sky." He diverted his eyes to the window and stared happily. "I am so glad you talked me into coming along with you. How can I thank you?"

Mark and Kate smiled at him. When the plane *hit a bump* or made a noise, they assured him everything was fine, and there was nothing to worry about. After two stops with layovers and twenty hours later, he was grateful they had reached their final destination at Ben Gurion Airport in Tel Aviv. As the plane approached, Jonathan took in the aerial view of the landscape below, which was more than he ever expected. His excitement grew every moment as the plane began its descent.

"Oh, wow, Internet photos do not do this place justice. I never realized how many trees we have in Vermont." Jonathan chuckled, and his friends patted him on the back, smiling at his innocent, child-like wonder. "I never imagined how fantastic everything looks in *real life*! It's desert for miles here, right? We are definitely *not* in Vermont!" Jonathan chuckled again.

He congratulated himself on surviving his first time flying; it felt good, and he smiled as they deboarded the plane.

Mark placed a hand on his shoulder as they walked down the gangway. "See? You did great. Easy peasy!"

"Thanks, you guys have been amazing; you two are the best friends a loser like me could have."

Kate gave him a gentle punch in the arm. "Stop saying stuff like that! You are *not* a loser!"

The three of them walked down the gangway arm in arm, laughing. *I'm so looking forward to this adventure,* Jonathan thought to himself.

Ben Gurion airport was much larger than he had expected.

"Did you guys notice all the soldiers carrying guns?"

"Yes. This is one of the most secure airports in the world. After several terrorist attacks in the past, there is extra security to keep people safe."

After clearing customs and immigration, the dig team met a representative from the Israel Antiquities Authority. He helped them get their gear on the minibus to take them to the youth hostel, where they would stay for three days while in Jerusalem.

Before boarding the bus, Reverend Hogan gathered the team around like a mother hen with her chicks. "Listen, this is very important. We are visitors to this country; I expect all of you to obey the rules and customs we went over in our meetings. We all must stay together, so no one gets lost. Is that understood?"

Jonathan and the others nodded in compliance. "Our three-day stay in Jerusalem will allow us to get acclimated to the climate, do some sightseeing, and visit sites mainly related to King Solomon. We will also visit the Israel Antiquities

Authority to submit our paperwork to the Israeli government." He looked around and made a point to make eye contact with each team member. "Okay, let's get on board the bus and head into the city."

Jonathan made sure he got one of the window seats to see everything on their forty-five-minute trip to Jerusalem. The minibus was very comfortable and easily held the U.S. dig team and all of their equipment. One of the first things Jonathan noticed was the air-conditioned bus, a new experience for him.

As they entered Jerusalem, Jonathan took in the incredible ancient structures and buildings, the cacophony of sounds from all the vehicles and the crowds of people, the bright colors of their clothing and unusual dress, the exotic smells of the food cooking, and the street vendors. He was amazed by this ancient city. It felt like he had been transported back in time to some mysterious, magical place.

"I can't believe this city has been here for thousands of years. It's amazing," he exclaimed.

Kate turned to Mark. "I've never seen him like this before; he's genuinely excited."

"Well, we'll see how excited he is when we are out in the desert in the heat, and he has to get his hands dirty."

"Oh!" She gave him a dirty look and an elbow jab to the ribs—he feigned pain and grimaced with a smile.

Mark was right. I guess this expedition could be like living inside an adventure game, finding clues, and putting an ancient puzzle together. It sure feels that way right now.

Fortunately, Jonathan liked puzzles.

He had never seen or imagined anything like this place. His mom ran through his mind, and instead of feeling sad, he smiled, thinking of how she'd love it that he could experience this drastic change from the small quiet hometown of Harrington that he always knew. Jonathan thought of the scene from *The Wizard of Oz* when Dorothy arrived in Oz, and everything changed from sepia to Technicolor. Her famous line from the film ran through his mind, "Toto, I have a feeling we're not in Kansas anymore!"

The dig team arrived at the youth hostel where they would stay while in Jerusalem. They unpacked their luggage and settled in for their stay. After a communal dinner with other young people staying at the hostel, Mark said, "I think I am going to head for bed. We've been going nonstop for a while. I'm totally bushed." Kate and Jonathan agreed. They wished him goodnight and headed for their beds as well. But despite the time change and constant going, Jonathan was too excited to fall asleep. He sat on the edge of his bunk and removed his journal from his backpack.

> I can't believe I'm really here! This is a fantastic place—much more than I could have ever imagined. Pictures don't do it justice. I am in a city that has existed for thousands of years. People from everywhere live here. It's bigger than I thought it would be with more people and more traffic. Everything is ancient and modern too. I'm so glad to be here.

As usual, writing helped him relax, and he fell asleep and woke the next morning excited for the day ahead. After breakfast, Reverend Hogan called them all together to discuss plans for sightseeing and their visit to the Israel Antiquities Authority.

"All right, listen up, everyone! On today's agenda, we'll visit several Biblical sites in and around Jerusalem. Please pay close attention to our guide, and try to get a feel for this city and its history. Once again, please stay together and don't wander off. The streets here can be confusing, and it would be easy to get lost. After lunch, we'll need to register our paperwork and meet the senior dig coordinator, Jedidiah Cohen, from the Israel Antiquities Authority. Mr. Cohen represents the Israeli government in charge of the dig with me."

Absorbed in the sightseeing trip, Jonathan enjoyed hearing this ancient city's history and seeing the sites connected to the fabled king.

"This place is like stepping into a history book," Jonathan said, remembering how he hated history in school. It was dull and boring, but this was *entirely* different. While exploring, he appreciated these were places he could never have imagined seeing.

In the afternoon, they went to the Israel Antiquities Authority to deliver their paperwork and meet Mr. Cohen. Jedidiah was a likable character, slightly overweight with a broad, confident face, a short, cropped gray beard, and a ring of short gray hair that circled his bald head. He made a point of greeting all the dig team members individually but briefly paused when he met Jonathan.

"And what's your name, young man?"

"My name is Jonathan Tobias, sir. It's genuinely nice to meet you."

"Yes, it is very nice to meet you as well, Jonathan Tobias."

For a second, Jonathan felt like Jedidiah's calm blue eyes drilled deeply into his soul; then, the fleeting feeling vanished. There was a gentle and knowing smile from Jedidiah. The brief encounter left Jonathan with a haunting yet overall peaceful feeling and connection to something he couldn't quite explain.

NINE

RESCUE

The next day, they did more sightseeing, sampled exotic food, and visited a bazaar. That evening after dinner at the hostel, Jonathan wanted to go outside for a few minutes.

"Hey, I'm going to step outside for fresh air before going to bed."

"Just remember to stay nearby, and don't wander off. Remember what Reverend Ken told us," Mark commented.

"Yes, *Dad*, I'll stay nearby," he said as he made his way outside. *I'm not some kind of baby.*

"Ooh, burn, Mark!" Kate cooed from the background with a smile.

He sat on the steps in front of the building for a few minutes, soaking in the fresh air. Then, he heard exotic music drifting through the wind. Intrigued by the melody, he followed the sound and thought maybe he'd find a bar for a quick drink. The exotic spices and street vendors' foods smelled heavenly. Ancient architecture in the old city caught his eye, and the unfamiliar people fascinated him. Jonathan forgot Reverend Ken's earlier warning and wandered off. He sought the source of the mysterious and haunting music as he took in his surroundings and ignored where he was going.

The streets twisted and turned, and before long, Jonathan realized he was lost. It gripped him with fear, and sheer panic swept over him. Every fearful thought or circumstance flashed through his mind. *What am I going to do?* He reached in his pocket for his phone. *Where's my phone? Oh, no! I left it in my other pants pocket!* Jonathan panicked, remembering he didn't speak the language or even know what direction he had taken.

He regretted his actions. *Why was I so stupid to go out alone in a strange city half way around the world? Me! I haven't been anywhere in my whole life! What was I thinking?*

Jonathan frantically tried to retrace his steps, but the city streets were confusing, as Reverend Hogan had warned. Jonathan turned around, but every street looked the same. What was beautiful and intriguing a few minutes ago had changed into a terrifying labyrinth. *Why are those people looking at me funny? Do those men over there want to harm me?* He stood on a street corner and looked around him in all directions. *How far have I gone?* Then, he ran in a panic. He darted down one street and then another, trying to recognize some landmark to guide him to safety.

He raced around yet another corner and ran full-on into someone who grabbed him by the arm. In a panic, Jonathan tried to get free. "Let me go! Let me go!"

But the stranger's grip tightened, and a voice said, "Jonathan? Jonathan Tobias?"

Jonathan stopped struggling and saw it was Jedidiah from the IAA. "Mr. Cohen?"

"Jonathan, are you alone?"

"Ah, yes, sir."

"What are you doing out wandering around the city? All of you knew to stay together and not wander off alone."

Jonathan blurted out, "I only wanted some fresh air. When I heard music and walked toward it, I stopped paying attention and got lost! I'm sorry." Embarrassed, Jonathan nearly hyperventilated.

RESCUE

Jedidiah put his hands on Jonathan's shoulders and looked him squarely in the eyes, and said, "Everything is all right now. You're okay. Calm down; take a breath." Jedidiah's voice was genuinely kind, comforting, and reassuring. He kept telling Jonathan he was safe instead of rebuking him. Jedidiah asked, "Would you like to share some tea with me? It will help calm your nerves. Oh, and please call me Jedidiah."

"Yes, I'd like that very much, sir. I mean, Jedidiah." Jedidiah smiled his now-familiar, mysterious smile.

He put his arm around Jonathan's shoulder as they walked a short distance to a little sidewalk café, and Jedidiah ordered them tea.

"Thank you."

"Oh, it is nothing."

"No, I mean, thank you for rescuing me. I was terrified. Wow, it is such a relief to literally run into you. I don't know what I would have done." Jonathan shifted his eyes down to the tabletop.

"Ah, yes, that *was* a lucky chance encounter." Jedidiah smiled. *For some strange reason, Jonathan didn't feel like it was a chance encounter.* "Yes, Jedidiah, I am very grateful."

Jedidiah explained, "Fear is natural; it is part of human nature. We should *not* run in panic but should confront the terror and deal with it calmly. Life holds many fears and doubts about ourselves. Do not run from them but confront them and learn from them. That is how we grow. However, when a lion is chasing you, then, by all means, *run!*" They both laughed, and Jonathan started to feel much better. Being with Jedidiah made him feel secure and relaxed.

Jonathan enjoyed the tea; it was not like any tea he had ever tasted before. This tea was exotic and fragrant and calmed his shattered nerves. "This tea tastes wonderful. It's *different*. I guess that's the best way to explain it."

"It is a special tea for calming the nerves. I'm glad you like it. Now, tell me, Jonathan Tobias, what brings you on this expedition? Why did you choose to seek knowledge about a famous Jewish king?"

"My friends talked me into coming with them. Kate's father, Reverend Hogan, organized the trip and the dig."

"Yes, I have known Reverend Kenneth for many years. He is an outstanding Biblical scholar. But why are you *really* here, Jonathan Tobias?" It was as if Jedidiah knew the secret in Jonathan's heart of hearts that to be someone special, you have to *do* something special.

"Well, as I said, I came with my friends. I thought it would be an adventure."

"Ah, an adventure, you say? I think maybe you have already begun your adventure this evening?"

"Yes, I guess I have. Haven't I?" Jonathan sheepishly smiled, expecting a tongue lashing for what he did. Instead, he received kindness and understanding, which were emotions he found unusual, especially from another man.

"And is an adventure your *only* reason?"

"Why, yes. What other reason would I have?"

"Possibly something more, I think." Jonathan once again felt those piercing blue eyes look deep within his heart.

"No, just adventure." He lied.

"So, tell me, what do you think of my city, Jonathan Tobias?"

Your city? But Jonathan dismissed the thought. "I live, or rather, *we all live* in a small town in Vermont. And I've never been this far from my home, so having the opportunity to be in this country is pretty amazing to me."

"Amazing! An interesting word to describe Israel and Jerusalem. This is a beautiful and ancient country and a city with a rich troubled history. Much has happened here. And you, my young friend, are here to uncover some of that history and are destined to find much more, I think."

Jonathan considered Jedidiah's last comment. *I wonder what he means.*

RESCUE

They sat for a while, drank their tea, and mainly talked about Jonathan and his life back home. His story spilled out of him like a bottle of shaken pop. He found it easy to speak with Jedidiah. Jonathan had never known how that felt—it was not like him to share his deepest hurts with a stranger like this before.

After a short time, Jedidiah walked Jonathan back to the hostel and cautioned him again about going off alone. "Remember, mind what I tell you and stay with the others, particularly while you are in the city."

"You can be sure that I have learned my lesson," he said with a smile.

"Well, then, Jonathan Tobias, I will say good night until we meet at the dig site."

"Good night, Jedidiah. Thank you again for the tea." They didn't mention Jedidiah rescuing Jonathan that evening but seemed to have an understanding between them.

"Good night again, my young friend." he bowed with a flourish and a smile.

Jonathan turned to repeat a good night, but Jedidiah was gone. *That's strange; he was just here a second ago, right behind me. Where did he go?* Jonathan looked around and shook his head, perplexed. He entered the building and felt a curious connection between them as he walked through the lobby to the stairs pondering the days ahead.

When he got to his room before going to sleep, he felt disturbed by the night's events and knew writing would help him sort through his feelings.

One of the scariest and strangest things happened to me tonight. I managed to get myself lost in the city because I was stupid and didn't obey the others' warnings about wandering off alone. And then, in my panic, out of nowhere, I ran into Mister Cohen—Jedidiah! Like all of a sudden, he was just there to rescue me. And instead of hollering at me for getting lost, he offered me tea to calm my nerves and wanted to know more about me. When we said good night a few minutes ago, I turned to look back, and he had disappeared. I have the strangest feeling that everything that happened tonight was not an accident, but it feels like I was supposed to get lost and run into Jedidiah . . .

TEN

THEIR ADVENTURE BEGINS—THE DIG

Jonathan didn't share the previous evening's events with any of the others. He felt embarrassed about going off alone and getting lost. But he also couldn't explain the sudden and surprising encounter with Jedidiah Cohen, which was still a mystery to him.

In the morning at breakfast, Mark asked, "Where were you last night?"

"I sat out on the front steps for a while. It was just a nice evening."

"Oh? Well, I was worried about you and went out there but didn't see you."

"Well, I walked around the corner to a café and had some tea. I needed to be by myself for a little while."

"Well, I'm glad you didn't get lost."

"No, I didn't get lost!" he replied sarcastically. *Oh, if he only knew!*

The dig team spent the final day in Jerusalem, gathering their gear getting ready for the dig.

It didn't take long for Jonathan to discover this adventure would not be a vacation. Sorting through the gear and repacking it turned out to be hard and grueling work in the brutal heat. He was not used to that kind of manual labor and complained. "I had no idea this was going to be so tricky repacking and arranging! This heat is murder!"

Mark was nearby and heard Jonathan. He responded, "Well, what did you think this was going to be, a picnic? I told you before we left home what we would be doing. Get it together, man, and stop your whining!"

Jonathan nodded, and for the rest of the day, he did not complain about anything but concentrated on the adventure ahead and what it would be like to find King Solomon's lost treasure. He visualized his fantasy. *I see myself standing in the middle of a room surrounded by gold and jewels as the one who discovered his ancient treasure. I'll be famous! That will show Dad!*

That evening, Jonathan was exhausted, and after dinner, he retired early for the evening. Still, the grandiose visions from earlier in the day flooded his mind as he fell asleep thinking about how great it would be to find the treasure and finally be someone special—someone famous.

The following day, the team assembled their gear and loaded it on the bus for the ninety-minute ride to the dig site outside Jerusalem. On the trip to the dig site, laughter and excitement bounced off the walls. Jonathan, Kate, Mark, and other members of the U.S. dig team were in high spirits.

Upon arrival at the dig site, Jedidiah met them and introduced them to the team's Israeli members. The Israelis were all graduate students from various universities in Israel. They had already been there for a day and had set up camp, ready to assist their U.S. team counterparts in unpacking their gear and getting organized and settled. There were fifteen dig members—nine males and six females—plus Reverend Hogan and Jedidiah.

THEIR ADVENTURE BEGINS—THE DIG

Jedidiah escorted the dig team around the site to familiarize them with the area and where they would be working. "As you can see, the site is extensive. We have only excavated about sixty percent of the entire structure and will concentrate our efforts on the southwest corner. By using ground-penetrating radar, we know there are several additional rooms located in that area."

Reverend Hogan added, "We will establish ten-foot by ten-foot grids in the area and will simultaneously work on one of these units, cataloging everything we find, marking its location within the grid. I'll go into more detail about the process as we begin, but for now, I want those of you not familiar with the excavation process to work closely with me. If you uncover anything unusual, you should contact Jedidiah or me before proceeding."

After the orientation with Jedidiah and Reverend Hogan, Jonathan spent the remainder of the day in his tent, then several hours exploring the dig site independently. Jedidiah said the site was extensive, but Jonathan had no idea what that meant until he studied it. He also made sure to familiarize himself with the tents near the dig location. It was awe-inspiring to walk through the ruins of a building inhabited three thousand years before. Not used to the desert conditions, it felt extra hot, dusty, and exhausting, but Jonathan was excited to be there.

That night, Jonathan felt the exertion of the day's activities; every muscle in his body ached, but he was in good spirits. Before going to dinner, he sat on his cot and wrote down his thoughts about the first day on the dig.

> *Today was hectic; I am totally exhausted but very excited about this expedition. It feels like it is going to be a real adventure. I walked around today and can't believe the size and how magnificent this place must have been. There had to have been hundreds of people who lived and worked here. There is nothing but desert for miles around. I wonder what*

it must have been like three thousand years ago. Well, I guess that's what we're here to discover. I have to admit the sleeping accommodations leave a bit to be desired, but I guess you can't have everything.

He left the tent and walked to the cook shack for dinner. He found Mark and Kate there, already making new friends with some of the Israeli team members. "May I join you guys?"

"Of course! Grab some food, and we'll move down and make room," Kate replied.

Kate introduced the others; she was always the social butterfly. The merriment of meeting new people and making friends made the evening pass quickly. On the other hand, Reverend Hogan and Jedidiah sat apart from the others, deep in discussion over maps and photographs, planning the dig.

The tents—their sleeping quarters—were large. Team members slept on cots in sleeping bags with their gear. The males bunked together, and the females bunked in the other tents.

Even though the days were sweltering in the desert, the nights were equally cold, another situation for which Jonathan was unprepared. To him, *camping* meant staying in a hotel with running water and indoor facilities. *Why didn't I ask more questions before I volunteered for this?* Jonathan questioned himself, remembering Mark's words. *Oh, it'll be an adventure. I'll remember that. Only seven weeks, three days to go.*

The second day of the dig started early, right after breakfast, laying out the grid for the area they'd work during the excavation. Jonathan found it interesting to use laser sighting devices to determine the locations of the gridded regions.

THEIR ADVENTURE BEGINS—THE DIG

He worked closely with Reverend Hogan as they surveyed the area. "This is pretty cool! I had no idea you used high-tech instruments in archaeology."

"Well, the field of archaeology has come a long way with many technological advances in recent years. It's *real* science now. You'll have plenty of opportunities to get sweaty and to get your hands dirty when we start excavating," he said with a grin.

Jonathan liked the high-tech equipment, and working with the other members of the team was fun. He learned a lot about the setup of an excavation site and how they determined where to dig through ground-penetrating radar and satellite photographs; all of the preparations were fascinating. He started to feel like he was part of a team, and they all worked toward a common goal. His selfish thoughts faded from his mind.

Mark pointed at Jonathan. "Look at Jon; I think he's enjoying himself."

"I wish you had more faith in him. This experience might be just what he needs to get on with his life," Kate said as she looked over at Jonathan.

"We'll see once the real work begins. I hope you're right."

It took the entire day for the team to establish and mark off the grid. Jedidiah and Reverend Ken supervised based on the photographs and documents they had discussed the night before.

The next day, the *real work* began. They carefully shoveled the top layers of dirt into buckets, sifted through their contents, and looked for anything of interest. Reverend Ken worked closely with the team members without previous dig experience—primarily the U.S. team members—specifically Kate, Jonathan, and Mark.

"Begin at the corner of the square; work along one edge and across the square to the other. Based on your area's photographs, carefully remove the top layer of dirt and put it in one of the buckets. We start with the shovels, then move to use a trowel, and finally, a wooden skewer and brush. It's all very methodical."

Mark asked, "What do we do when we find something that looks interesting, sir?"

"The first thing to do is to note the location of the object and record its position in the grid before removing it for cataloging. You all have cell phones, so it will be a simple matter to photograph it. We'll be looking for anything to give us additional information about who built and lived in this grand palace."

Reverend Ken said it with such emotion; his words inspired Jonathan. He hadn't thought of it that way before. "So, what you're saying, sir, is we're looking for answers to a mystery time has almost erased. And it's our job to find the clues and solve the mystery."

"Yes, you're correct; that is a great way to explain it."

Suddenly, he felt like he had a purpose for being there, and it felt good, no matter what the crummy living conditions were.

At first, it was back-breaking work, but his body conditioned in a short time, and the tasks became more natural. Strangely for Jonathan, the work didn't feel monotonous or tedious like working in the mailroom or like any of the other jobs he had before.

He quickly learned the process of carefully excavating to uncover traces of a possible story. *What would the next shovel of dirt reveal?* Jonathan felt like he was digging for buried treasure, and he had memories of books about pirate adventures he read as a child. Time had hidden the treasure, and once again, he was determined to find it. His thoughts of finding something valuable, special, a precious prize—*finding Solomon's riches*—all resurfaced.

Before they left home, Jonathan took some time to read Bible verses and information on the Internet about Solomon, but the ones about his wealth and power interested him the most. **"King Solomon was greater in riches and wisdom** than all the other kings of the earth. All the kings of the earth sought audience with Solomon to hear the wisdom God had put in his heart" (2 Chronicles 9:22–23). "Wealth and riches are in his house, and his righteousness endureth forever" (Psalm 112:3). Sure, he was wise, but that was what brought him riches, glory, and power. Jonathan never knew these things but dreamed of possessing them.

Day after day, they dug and sorted through pottery sherds and bits of clay, looking for clues of something to add relevance to the Reverend's research. They noted and cataloged all they found. For Jonathan, it was like putting together an ancient jigsaw puzzle. The pieces were there; he had to find them and figure out where they fit in the puzzle to tell the story. He remembered the first time he found one of the pottery sherds and what it was like to uncover it and how it felt to hold something in his hand another person had held over three thousand years prior. It thrilled him.

"Hey, guys, take a look at what I just found."

"Good job! Now, you need to see if it fits with any of the others."

"I'm going to check it out right now."

Later that night, he wrote.

I found my first pottery sherd today. It was amazing to hold it in my hand and turn it over, knowing another person thousands of years ago held the vessel that this sherd belongs to. I wonder who they were. What were they like? What did they do in this grand palace? This place holds so many unanswered questions.

He found the whole process fascinating, and the more he did, he grew in his skills. Since that first discovery, there had been many sherds. Each one still excited him, and it brought him closer to solving the puzzle. He enjoyed the praise from Reverend Ken and Jedidiah on his keen eye, astute observations, his ability to make sense of the broken sherds, and the story they told of the people who lived there. Unfortunately, they had yet to find anything conclusive regarding Solomon.

"Look at these two sherds, Jedidiah. I think these match up with those I found a couple of days ago in grid twenty-three; these are in twenty-one. What do you make of that?"

"I think you need to keep digging, Jonathan. You're on to something, but you need to find a link between their locations."

"They definitely are part of the same vessel, but why are they so far apart?"

"See if there are any other sherds located in twenty-two that fit. Great job connecting them. You've got a good eye for this."

"Thanks!"

Jonathan thought how great it felt to have someone appreciate something he'd done. *I don't think that has ever happened to me before. Wonders never cease!*

That night before going to sleep, Jonathan recounted the day.

> *Wow! I received a compliment from Jedidiah today. I think that is the most encouraging thing anyone has ever said to me. He told me I had a good eye for this and piecing the sherds together. I didn't realize how great it would feel to receive a compliment for something. It just hasn't ever happened before! It feels really, really good! I know I am going to find that treasure! It's only a matter of time!*

Over the coming days, Mark and Kate also noticed the gradual change in Jonathan.

"What's gotten into him over the past couple of weeks?" Mark asked.

"I don't know, but I like whatever it is. Jon is a different person. I've never seen him as interested in something or as driven when doing anything except for a good computer video game," Kate said.

"Hm, maybe he is pretending it's some computer game," Mark pondered.

"No, I don't think so. I think Jon is genuinely interested. It seems like he likes archaeology."

"Oh, please, I haven't seen him *really* interested in anything—besides computer games—since we were kids."

"I think you're mistaken. He enjoys finding objects and putting them together like a giant puzzle."

"Maybe you're right. It's good to see Jon engaged and interested in something other than himself. You might be right. This trip could be a good thing for him, after all."

"I'm pretty certain it has. The other day, I overheard my dad talking to Jedidiah about the great job Jon is doing and his obvious interest in archaeology."

"Well, that would be a blessing, for sure. It's draining to listen to him complain about how miserable he is all the time. What a nice break to see him excited and involved for a change."

"Come on. Give him a break. You know his home life and the trouble in school and how everyone teased him," Kate offered.

"Yeah, yeah. I know kids in school were pretty horrible to him. Honestly, the teachers weren't much better. Jon *is* doing a great job here. Your dad was worried he would be a problem."

"Well, it looks like he was wrong about that; I'm glad," Kate replied.

Jonathan was more determined than ever to find Solomon's treasure and become famous. He poured over the site maps and satellite photographs, trying desperately to see something to lead him to clues that might help him find the buried treasure. He noticed an anomaly in grid thirty-two, but it would have to wait until later to explore.

ELEVEN

DISCOVERY

The team entered their fourth week of the dig and made some significant discoveries. Though they found bits of clay tablets and clay seals, the inscriptions were damaged and incomplete. It appeared the site had experienced a major catastrophic incident of some type, possibly an earthquake or destruction by foreign armies. Still, there hadn't been anything conclusive to determine who constructed the massive site, but the work progressed steadily. Absorbed in the project, and because of Jedidiah's guidance, Jonathan learned a lot about archaeology. Jonathan thought of Jedidiah and Reverend Ken as mentors willing to share their knowledge with him. He was grateful for what he learned from them and their friendship, which he hadn't experienced from older men.

One evening before bed, Jonathan took out his journal and wrote down his feelings about what the past few days had been like.

> I have been learning so much from Jedidiah and Reverend Ken. I've never known bosses like either of them. They both are so willing to share their knowledge with me and encourage me to do better. I've never had a boss praise my work before and make me feel like I was actually doing a good job. They are kind and treat me with respect. Sometimes, it is tough for

me to believe what they are saying is really true. I mean, I can tell they're being honest with their kind words and votes of confidence. But it feels weird. I was thinking about why it is tough for me to believe what they say. And it occurred to me that my dad and old man Jacobs never gave me credit.

Jedidiah called Jonathan over to his tent one afternoon; Reverend Ken was also there. It made Jonathan uneasy. *Oh boy, what's wrong?*

"Come in and sit down, Jonathan." Jedidiah pointed to a chair.

"Is something wrong? Did I screw something up?"

"What makes you think something is wrong?" Reverend Ken asked.

"Every time someone's called me into the boss's office, it's because I messed something up."

The Reverend chuckled. "No, you haven't messed anything up. On the contrary, we'd like to promote you to a team leader position on the dig. We've noticed your diligence here. You show focus, determination, and perhaps without realizing it, you already tend to lead the others to stay on task."

"What? Really! You're not kidding me, are you?"

"No, we're not kidding." He chuckled again. "You'll be leading the team with Mark, Kate, Ruth, and Aaron."

"Oh, wow! This is fantastic!" Jonathan hopped up, excited.

"Just make sure your friendship with Mark and Kate doesn't get in the way of the work."

"No, sir, I won't! I hope Mark and Kate won't be angry. Do you think they'll feel weird I'm now in charge of the team?"

"I don't think you need to worry about that," Reverend Ken said.

Jonathan left in a hurry to tell Kate and Mark the news.

Jedidiah remarked, "I think this is good for Jonathan. The promotion will allow him to learn some things about himself—what it takes to be a team leader, working with others, doing a good job, praising others for a job well done, relying on others for help and guidance, discovering the value of developing friends, and practicing responsibility—for starters."

"You're right. He needed to start feeling like others could rely on him. That's a new concept to him, and he deserved the responsibility. I think he has a natural aptitude for the work."

"You are correct; this young man has a natural feel for the work and an inquisitive mind."

Jonathan found Mark and Kate working in one of the grids. "Hi, guys! How's it going?"

"Pretty good. We found a couple more of those pottery sherds. What's up?" Kate replied.

"I had a conversation with your dad and Jedidiah. They promoted me to lead our team. I hope that's okay with you guys?" Jonathan said.

They jumped up and gave him high-fives. "Well, of course, it is! We've considered you to be the team leader for weeks. Not a problem with us. Who will be working with us?"

"Ruth and Aaron are the other members," Jonathan replied.

"Oh, that's cool. I like them! We'll make an outstanding team," Kate added with a nod.

Jonathan told them, "We'll be working in grids thirty-one, thirty-two, and thirty-three for the next few days. We might find some interesting objects. From the aerial photos, it looks like one of the kitchens might have been in that area. Maybe we can locate more of those pottery sherds. Also, I noticed there might be an anomaly in grid thirty-two from the ground-penetrating radar images."

That night, before falling asleep, Jonathan jotted down thoughts in his journal.

Apparently, I have skills I never realized I had, and others are noticing me and recognizing my skills. I'm not stupid or good for nothing! I'm beginning to see for myself how wrong my father was—dead wrong! I'm not a screw-up! Important people trust and value me.

As he looked at the canvas above his head, he allowed these positive thoughts to sink into his mind. With those life-giving thoughts, he drifted off into a peaceful sleep, feeling better than he had ever felt.

∞

A couple of days later, Jonathan's team worked together near one of the exposed interior walls connected with another, forming the corner of grid thirty-two inside the ruin. Suddenly, Jonathan's shovel struck something hard, but it wasn't where there should have been a hard surface. *Here's my anomaly.* He carefully removed more dirt and sand and revealed the edge of what appeared to be a large, rectangular stone. It was smooth and polished, not like the rougher stone in the adjacent walls, and had a slightly worn area in the center.

Jonathan called over to the others. "Hey, guys, what do you make of this?"

"That's odd. Why would a stone that size and shape be next to and perpendicular to a wall?" Kate asked.

"Why would a stone that shape and size be *anywhere* inside the wall at all?" Mark added.

While the others watched, Jonathan carefully removed more dirt from around the stone. He discovered another one at the end, perpendicular to the first and parallel to the wall. "You guys try uncovering more stones in that direction." He pointed in a straight line toward the other wall.

As they carefully removed the earth, they found several more stones forming a straight line that ended at the opposite wall. Jonathan said, "I think we better let Jedidiah and

DISCOVERY

Reverend Ken know about this before we do anything else. Would one of you guys run and get them?"

Aaron ran off to get Jedidiah and Reverend Ken. Jonathan stood there, scratching his head. "What do you make of it? It's a large rectangle of stones in the sand."

"I don't have any idea," Kate commented.

"How about you, Mark?"

"You got me, buddy. I have no idea what it means or why it's here."

They stood there, puzzled and confused by the large rectangle made of stones emerging from the sand. What did it mean, and why was it located in the corner of that room?

TWELVE

TREASURE

Soon, Jedidiah and Reverend Ken arrived to examine what the team had discovered.

"What do you think it means?" Jonathan asked Jedidiah.

"I'm not quite sure what to make of it, Jonathan, but I think what you and your team discovered might be something quite important." Jonathan's pulse increased. He felt his heart in his throat. *Hm, something quite important!*

Jedidiah and Reverend Ken examined the rectangular space and talked for a few minutes.

Jedidiah looked at Jonathan and said, "I want your team to carefully excavate inside the stone perimeters. Start with the one you located first."

Mark asked Jedidiah, "Inside the stones? What do you think it is?"

"I'm not positive, but I think you might have discovered a staircase. Excavating inside the area defined by the stones will tell us if my assumption is correct."

Reverend Ken agreed, "So, let's get to it." With that, Jonathan entered the rectangle and carefully excavated the area next to the first stone.

After a short while, Jonathan uncovered a second stone about eight inches below the first. It was the same size and shape and met at the side of another stone perpendicular to it. "I think it *is* a step, Reverend Ken!"

The other members of the team joined Jonathan inside the rectangle to expedite the process.

Within an hour, they confirmed it was, in fact, a staircase filled in with dirt and rubble over the centuries. They uncovered the top two steps, a portion of the staircase wall, and the top edge of what appeared to be a door.

"Huh, it's a set of steps! "What do you think it goes to, Dad?" Kate leaned on her shovel, puzzled.

Before he could respond, Jonathan jumped up and exclaimed, "A treasure room!"

Reverend Hogan lifted one eyebrow. "What? I doubt that very much, Jonathan."

"Why not?"

"The physical location of an underground room in this area of the site isn't right."

"What? What do you mean?"

"Well, this area is far from the central area of the site. It's not in one of the main rooms. So, it's unlikely we'd encounter anything valuable in this location or underground, for that matter. It's certainly not a treasure room, Jonathan, but it definitely goes down to *something*. Let's keep digging, but be extremely careful; we don't know how stable these surrounding structures are. Jedidiah and I will need to examine these upper walls more closely to confirm their structural integrity."

"I'm going to contact my office and get a couple of our specialists out here tomorrow. They should be on site when we uncover whatever is at the bottom of this staircase," Jedidiah added.

Jonathan's heart pounded with excitement at the thought of finding buried treasure, even though he understood it was unlikely. He refused to let himself believe otherwise. His gut told him they'd find gold and jewels in the room at the bottom of the stairway.

TREASURE

Darkness halted the excavation for the day. The excitement was high in the camp that evening. After they cleaned up, Jonathan and his team entered the cook shack to eat dinner. The other dig team members cheered, hugged them, patted them on their backs, and gave high fives.

"Good going, Jonathan. It looks like you and your team might have found something worthwhile," someone said.

"Your keen eye saw that stone and led to the discovery," Jedidiah added.

Jonathan tried to be humble and share the glory, but he really wanted to take all the credit. *This treasure room discovery was mine. The others happened to be there at the same time. I was the one who saw the anomaly from the aerial photographs.*

That night, it was almost impossible for Jonathan to sleep; his excitement was virtually unbearable. He finally sat up on the side of his cot and began to write.

> *I knew I was going to be the one to discover the treasure room. I just knew it! No matter what Reverend Ken says, I'm confident the room will be filled with treasure, and I'll be the one who discovered it. I'll be famous. It was only a matter of time before my luck was gonna change, and I'd finally get a break! This is gonna be great! I can't wait for tomorrow to see what is buried in that room. Big time, here I come!*

Eventually, he did fall asleep from exhaustion and dreamt of piles of gold and jewels.

The next morning, after woofing down scrambled eggs, bacon, and coffee, Jonathan hurried back to the staircase excavation site. His team was already back at work.

"How is everything going?"

With a big smile, Mark hollered up from the excavation, "Great! We got started a little early, but we left you a lot more earth to sift through, so get down in this hole and help us!"

Jonathan climbed down into the excavation, and Mark handed him a shovel.

Reverend Hogan and Jedidiah were there to supervise. They worked slowly, careful not to miss anything important as they cleared the dirt and rubble. The team excavated far enough to reveal the top third of the door, which was very promising.

"There is a closed-door down here," Mark yelled up from the hole.

Other members of the dig team came to see what Jonathan's team had uncovered.

As the team dug further down, they found large stones and more substantial rubble pieces in the stairwell.

"What do you make of this, Reverend Ken? Where did these large stones come from, and why are they here? It looks like more stones are blocking the rest of the stairs. I think we're going to need more help getting these removed," Jonathan asked.

"There could have been a bad earthquake, and that's what caused them to abandon this site. Keep digging. I'll talk to Jedidiah and find out if he knows anything about an earthquake."

The two specialists from the Israel Antiquities Authority arrived and conferred with Jedediah and Reverend Hogan. As the team uncovered more of the stairs, the area size decreased with more door exposure. After locating the rectangle of stone, they took photos to document the progress of the excavation. Now, the specialists examined the partially exposed door itself, which appeared intact after thousands of years.

One of the specialists commented, "This is amazing; I can't believe this timber door is in such a preserved state."

"Possibly cedar—it's incredibly resistant to decay, but we'll need to run tests," the other said.

Jonathan grew anxious as they cleared more of the rubble from the stairs. They uncovered most of the door. He pictured all of the riches only inches away now. Jonathan felt like they were so close. They climbed the stairs—stairs that hadn't seen the light of day for nearly three thousand years. The entire dig team stood around the staircase, amazed at the discovery.

Jedidiah, Reverend Hogan, and the two specialists went down the stairs to examine the door and determine the best way to attempt to open it.

"Why didn't the walls caving in destroy the door too? There were stones and rubble piled against it," Reverend Hogan asked.

Jonah, one of the specialists from the IAA, replied, "This thing must be at least four inches thick. It's only received minor damage."

"Well, let's see if we can push it open. It might be blocked from the inside if whatever is behind it collapsed in the quake," Reverend Hogan said.

After more discussion, Reverend Hogan put his shoulder against the door and gave it a strong push. There was a slight movement; then the others pushed on it again, and it began to move. They opened it about eighteen inches, and Jedidiah handed Reverend Hogan a flashlight.

"Well, this is what you've come all this way for; you should be the first one in." Jedidiah put his hand on Reverend Hogan's shoulder and gave him a big, encouraging smile.

"Thanks for allowing me to go in first."

"This could be the end of a long search for you, my friend. Mazel Tov!"

He entered through the narrow space, followed by the others.

Everyone stood around the stairwell so quietly you could hear a pin drop; the excitement and anticipation were almost electrifying. Jonathan felt about to crawl out of his skin. He fidgeted and stuffed his hands in his pockets to simmer down as he thought he had found the lost treasure of Solomon.

He mumbled under his breath, "Come on, what's down there? What's in the room? What's taking so long? Why are they making us wait out here? I can't stand this."

Kate and Mark looked at him. "Calm down. They want to make sure it's safe, and the whole place doesn't cave in," Kate said.

He replied brusquely, "If it hasn't collapsed in three thousand years, opening the door isn't going to cause it to now!"

Kate looked at him, shocked. Mark wondered why Jon talked to Kate in that tone of voice.

THIRTEEN

INTO THE DEPTHS

Thirty minutes passed before Reverend Hogan emerged from the room. He looked up at the young men and women staring down at him with various expressions of confusion, anticipation, excitement, and questions on their faces.

He spoke in a humble tone, and his voice cracked. With tears in his eyes, he announced, "We have found a treasure of incalculable value!" He broke down sobbing as he slowly sat down on the lower steps and cried with joy.

Jonathan yelled down, "What kind of treasure?"

"You'll all have a chance to see for yourselves after the authorities finish photographing the room." In a few moments he stood, wiped the tears from his eyes, and re-entered the room.

The rest of the team wandered off to do other things while Jedidiah, Reverend Ken, and the specialists remained in the room. Jonathan didn't go anywhere. He paced back and forth near the edge of the staircase, hands in his pockets, with a determined look on his face. Then, he sat for a short time on the nearby rocks before he paced again. A tense two hours passed as he waited impatiently. *Why are they making me wait so long? This is driving me crazy! I want to see my treasure!*

Finally, Jedidiah and the two men from the IAA exited the room with Reverend Ken; they talked amongst themselves and reviewed photographs on their phones as they climbed the stairs.

With hands on his hips and tapping his foot, Jonathan asked, "When can we see the treasure? *I* found it, and I'd like to see it."

Reverend Ken and Jedidiah stopped and gave Jonathan a surprised glance, "Your team discovered the chamber, Jonathan, and we will be ready to let the rest of you see the contents in a little while."

They turned and walked away, leaving him standing there.

"What's gotten into you, talking to them like that? How rude!" Mark exclaimed.

"Well, why are they making us wait so long to see what's down there?"

"Because there is a protocol they have to follow before unauthorized individuals can enter the site; that's why! After all the time you've been here, you should understand the importance of documenting everything. We can't contaminate the site."

"I understand, but why is it taking so long?"

"It's only been a couple of hours. I am certain they want to make sure they've documented correctly and photographed everything."

"Fine! Whatever!"

Mark walked away, puzzled and disappointed. He met with Kate and shook his head. "I don't know what's gotten into him. He's acting like Dr. Jekyll and Mr. Hyde. One minute he is *part of the team*, and the next, he acts like an impatient child. I just don't get it."

Jonathan sat on one of the large stones piled near the entrance. He tapped his foot on the ground, waiting impatiently to enter the room. Jedidiah and the specialists brought portable lights and other equipment into the room.

INTO THE DEPTHS

Soon, Jedidiah came out, "All right, we are all set up down there so you can enter the room, one person at a time. Do not disturb anything while you are there. Jonah and Daniel are there and will answer any of your questions."

Jonathan jumped up to be first. Everyone on the team knew it was best to let him go first after the way he'd been acting.

"Go ahead," Jedidiah said, nodding. He motioned for him to go down the stairs to the room. Jonathan bounded down the steps two at a time and rushed into the room.

There was a moment of silence, and then he screamed, "No, No, *No*! This can't be right. Where is the treasure? What have you done with it?" He rushed up from the room to Jedidiah. He grabbed the front of Jedidiah's shirt in desperation and exclaimed, "Where's the treasure, Jedidiah? Where is it?"

With a knowing look, Jedidiah removed and held Jonathan's hands. In a calm voice, he said, "It's down there in the room, Jonathan."

"No, it isn't. There's nothing but a bunch of old junk in there! Where is Solomon's gold? Reverend Ken said there was a treasure down there worth *millions*."

"I don't think he or anyone else said anything about gold. But the contents of that room are valuable beyond imagination; they are priceless, and *you* are part of this discovery."

Jonathan wrenched himself free of Jedidiah's grip. "I can't believe this is happening!" He dropped to the ground and beat his fists against the dry earth. Jedidiah bent down and tried to comfort him, but Jonathan shrugged off his gesture. "Leave me alone!" he snapped. He got up, turned, and said, "I don't need your pity!" And he ran off toward the camp and beyond.

Everyone on the dig team watched Jonathan's outburst. There was a mixture of horror, questions, and disbelief.

Mark looked at Kate and said, "What just happened?"

She stood open-mouthed and shocked. But she managed to reply, "I have *absolutely* no idea! I've never seen him act like that."

"Well, if you ask me, I think he has fricking lost it big this time! All these weeks, we thought he had changed. But that person left the moment he didn't get what *he* wanted."

"Stop it. You know he hoped to find some *ridiculous* treasure."

"Uh, excuse me, what did we just discover if it isn't a treasure?"

"He doesn't see it that way right now."

"Yeah, and he never will either. He's too thick-headed to understand anything. Honestly, I've just about had enough of all his bull!"

Jedidiah excused himself and walked toward the camp. Kate remarked as he walked away, "I hope he can talk some sense into him."

"Don't count on it," Mark replied.

Jonathan stomped through the camp and out into the desert beyond. He found himself standing at the edge of a ledge overlooking the vastness of the solitary desert. The view gave him a sense of solitude. This was a place where he could see things from a higher viewpoint, which he needed right now. He stood there for a moment scratching his head in disbelief, and then sat down on the ledge and cupped his head in his hands. *How is this real? I was so sure there would be a treasure, something unique, something to make me fam*ous. *My father always said I was a loser; I guess he's right. After all the hard work here, I only found old clay jugs, containers, and some crummy old tools.* "There wasn't anything special—anything valuable. I tried to get with the program to show I could do something right. But in the end, it didn't mean a thing. I didn't find Solomon's riches."

INTO THE DEPTHS

Jedidiah heard a voice on the wind and found Jonathan sitting on the ledge. He approached him. "Jonathan, may I speak with you?"

"Jedidiah, I don't want to talk to anyone right now, please."

"I think this is important, and we need to talk now."

"*Fine*!" Jonathan moved over so Jedidiah could sit next to him.

"I know you are disappointed not to find a gold-filled room. I understand, but you need to realize the room *does* contain things far more valuable than gold, jewels, or any monetary treasure."

"Nothing is more valuable than gold, Jedidiah! Solomon was rich; he had wealth and power. Finding that would have made me famous like Howard Carter when he found Tutankhamun's tomb. It was full of gold and cool stuff."

Jedidiah shook his head in disbelief and disappointment. "So, Jonathan, in your mind, the point of archaeology is finding hidden treasure? In all the conversations we have had these past weeks, you didn't understand we were here attempting to uncover the past and learn more about who lived here? That's what archaeology is all about. It's *not* about finding treasure."

"Yeah, sure. But I was hoping to find something special."

"What? Something special?"

"Yeah, like treasure and riches!"

"What *is* your idea of treasure and riches, Jonathan?"

"Gold and jewels and stuff like that!"

Frustrated, Jedidiah took a deep breath. "Jonathan, this discovery is big, *monumental*! You and your team found valuable things in terms of their historical, religious, and scientific values. We cannot put a dollar amount on the knowledge these objects will provide. You *did* find a treasure, Jonathan. It's still too early to determine how significant, but it *is* extraordinary!"

"I got it, I got it. Can you please leave me alone? I don't want to talk about it anymore." Jedidiah got up and walked away in dismay at Jonathan's attitude, shaking his head.

Mark and Kate had their chance to observe the room's contents and were amazed at what it held: completely intact storage containers bearing Solomon's seal, some copper tools, and sealed clay cylinders thought to contain papyrus scrolls. There was no doubt it was a storage room. The fantastic thing was how well preserved everything was for over three thousand years. "I understood why my dad broke down in tears when he entered the room. He realized his life's dream; only time would tell how monumental this discovery is. I'm so happy for him."

"Yeah, it's pretty amazing for the whole team," Mark added. "I don't understand why Jon can't see that. Why is he acting like such a jerk? I thought he was getting his act together over the past few weeks. But I guess I was mistaken. He's still the same self-centered, unsatisfied mess, and the same complaining—it has to be all about me—jerk!"

"Please, come on, Jon is our friend."

Mark shoved his hands in his pockets in disgust and kicked at a rock in the dirt, "I know, but sometimes I get so sick and tired of his behavior and complaints about everything when stuff doesn't go *his* way. You realize he acted like a spoiled child when he discovered the room didn't contain gold. He threw a temper tantrum! Jon got down and literally beat his fists on the ground! It was embarrassing to watch!"

"I think we need to give Jon some space right now to process what's happened. Maybe he'll realize how amazing this find is."

They agreed to join the others and continue work.

That night, Jonathan sulked in his tent away from the others. His journal entry reflected his disappointment and anger.

INTO THE DEPTHS

Why can't I ever get a break? I thought this trip would be the turning point for me to have something to show for all my hard work and effort. This really sucks! And what's worse, no one, not even Mark and Kate, have a clue about how I feel and what doing something important and being someone important means to me. I hoped this trip and finding Solomon's riches would be the thing to change my life forever. Me—I'd be someone important and someone special and make my dad proud! Fat chance!

There was a lot of excitement around the camp over the discovery. Additional scientists from the IAA showed up at the site to help, and some journalists were interested in the story. Jonathan made himself scarce for the next two days as the crews photographed and cataloged the room's objects. He ate alone and didn't associate with anyone. Reverend Ken and Jedidiah attempted to encourage him to work with the IAA experts cataloging, preparing, and packing the objects for transport to their laboratory, but he wasn't interested.

Jonathan continued to act like a spoiled child who didn't get the present he wanted at Christmas. So, everyone stayed away, even Mark and Kate. They didn't have the time or energy to deal with his childish behavior.

There was still a lot of work to accomplish during the remaining time in Israel. The next few days were difficult for Jonathan. The dig hadn't stopped since discovering the room. He was still a team leader and had to work with the other team members. Everyone witnessed his verbal outburst at Jedidiah and tantrum when he realized the room wasn't full of gold like he thought. Naturally, he was embarrassed by his behavior in front of everyone, so he kept his distance and interacted with others only when he had to. Jonathan begrudgingly did his part, but Jedidiah could tell he still didn't grasp the discovery's importance and his role in it.

One morning after breakfast, Kate approached her father's tent and asked if she could interrupt and speak with him. "Sure, honey, I always have time to talk to you. What's going on?"

"It's about Jonathan. I'm beginning to worry about him."

"How so?"

"Well, I've never seen him acting the way he is now. I know he has problems, but he's never behaved like this in all the years I've known him."

"I expressed my concerns before we came on the trip. Jonathan has some real problems, Kate, but I don't think there is anything you or anyone else can do to help this time. He is simply going to have to deal with his issues."

"Are you sure? Maybe I should try talking to him and attempt to help him understand the importance of the discovery and his part in it."

Reverend Hogan took his glasses off, put them on his portable desk, pulled his daughter close, and kissed her on the forehead. "Listen, Kate, do you remember the time when you were about eight years old and found the baby bird had fallen out of its nest, and you wanted to save it?"

Kate smiled at the memory. "Yeah."

"Well, you're trying to do that again, my dear. It didn't work then; I don't think it's going to work this time either. You're always trying to fix things, make things better, and help people; that's why you'll be such a great nurse and why I love you so much. Take my word for it. Jonathan needs to work through this on his own."

"Okay, I understand. So, I need to stay out of it." Comprehension dawned on her as she hugged her dad. "Thanks for the advice."

INTO THE DEPTHS

On the third afternoon after the discovery, Jonathan saw Kate sitting in the shade of one of the tents drinking bottled water and taking a break. He approached and asked if he could join her.

"Sure. Grab some water and sit." She was incredibly happy for her father that his dig turned out to be much more than he could have ever imagined.

He sat next to her and grabbed a bottle of water. "I'm glad this has been a success for your dad. He's a great guy."

"Yeah, I am very happy for him too; this is the culmination of his lifelong dream." She looked at him and saw he was disappointed and hurt. "I'm sorry it wasn't what you were expecting to discover—your dream." Trying to console him, she leaned forward and placed her hand on his knee. "Jon, we made history with this discovery. *You've* made history. You found the staircase! This is all because of *you*!" Kate's words fell on deaf ears.

"Why are you trying to make me feel better about this?" Jonathan asked.

"Because!"

"Huh? What do you mean?"

She jumped up from her seat, threw her arms around his neck, and kissed him. It wasn't a *friendly* kiss but a full passionate, lover's kiss. She released him and sat back down, shocked at what she had done.

"What? What was that about?"

She smiled, embarrassed, and started to cry. "Because, you silly fool, I've been in love with you since the sixth grade. I love you! But you've been so self-absorbed and wallowing in your life problems you never noticed! I'm sorry you are disappointed we didn't find what you wanted, but I care about you! That's what it's all about!"

Jonathan was totally shocked. Mark saw them kiss. He considered turning around, but seeing they spotted him, he walked over to them.

He said, "Well, it's taken you two long enough to figure things out! It took six thousand miles, a foreign country, and a significant archaeological discovery. Geez." Mark turned to Jonathan. "It was pretty obvious that Kate has loved you from afar for most of your life, but you were too blind to see it."

Indeed, Jonathan was blindsided by what had happened. He raised his hands as if to protect himself, jumped up, knocked the chair backward, and hurried off into the desert and away from camp without saying anything. Kate and Mark stood surprised.

"Oh, no. What have I done?" she said. Mark put his arm around her shoulder and tried to comfort her as they watched Jonathan run away again.

"He's such a fool!" Mark responded.

"Where is he going?"

"Running from something he can't deal with like he always has!"

FOURTEEN

THE TRUE DISCOVERY

Jonathan got as far away from Kate and Mark as he possibly could. He staggered, lost and confused in the solitary and lonely wasteland. He screamed to the wind, "What's just happened? What? What!"

Jonathan's world had been thrown into complete chaos by Kate's profession of love. He tried to comprehend everything that had happened. *I've never thought of her that way. She's like a sister to me! I'm not ready to love someone! Sure, I like Kate, and I've known her forever, but love? Besides, this is about me and what I want.* He paced around in circles. His mind turned away from the awkward kiss with Kate and back to the dig. *I came on this trip expecting to find lost treasure, something unique to make me famous. Instead, I discovered a room full of old clay jugs and other old stuff? What kind of wealth is that? I thought Solomon was supposed to be rich! Whether this stuff has meaning for a bunch of scientists and history guys doesn't matter because it's not going to make me famous or important. I can't deal with that and Kate right now.*

He kicked a rock and looked up to the sun. "Kate is my friend and someone to talk to about how I'm feeling. And she dropped the *love* bombshell? To make things worse, my best friend has known about it and never said anything? I can't believe this!" He kicked at the ground and coughed when it raised a cloud of dust. "Have I been so blinded by *my* stuff not to realize what is going on around me? Within the last few days, both my friends have told me that!"

Jonathan returned to his tent and reached for his journal to set down on paper what was going through his mind.

> *I feel lost and unsure of anything right now. My purpose in this trip halfway around the world was to search for something to give my life meaning. And then, I made a discovery but not enough to make me famous. But I made new friends and found men who believed in and trusted me. And then Kate tells me she has been in love with me secretly for years. All of this has changed my life forever. I just can't deal with it. Am I really so wrapped up in myself that I can't see what's going on around me? What is happening to me? Nothing seems real anymore. I was so sure about everything. Now, I'm not so sure about anything. I need to talk to someone objective—I need to find Jedidiah.*

Jonathan left his tent to search for Jedidiah. He saw him sitting alone and asked, "May I join you? I need to talk to someone."

"Of course, please share my rock and fire." He motioned for Jonathan to sit beside him.

Jedidiah knew something was wrong and saw Jonathan was distraught. "What is it that's bothering you, my young friend?"

"First of all, I wanted to apologize for my behavior the other day. It was inappropriate. I am very sorry I acted the way I did, particularly since you were only trying to help."

"It's understandable. You were disappointed because you hoped for treasure, but instead, you found riches far beyond anything money can buy—even though you still don't understand that fact."

"Something happened today, and it turned my world upside down. I don't know how to deal with it."

"Sometimes, an objective point of view can help," Jedidiah said.

Ahh, just what Jonathan wanted to hear. He always found Jedidiah easy to talk to, so he explained, "Kate told me she loves me."

"What?"

Jedidiah didn't expect that to be the cause of Jonathan's moodiness, so a slight smile crossed his face. He said, "Well, Jonathan, why is someone loving you so difficult for you to believe?"

"I don't know; it just is. Plus, I've known Kate for years. I have never thought of her that way. She has always been a good friend since we were kids."

"Do you think anyone has ever loved you?" Jedidiah asked.

"My mom loved me, for sure. Since her death, all I have is Mark and Kate. My father hates me," Jonathan said sadly.

"Why do you think that?"

"I overheard him tell my mom during an argument when I was a kid. He said he never wanted me." Jonathan's voice cracked with emotion as he remembered that painful moment.

Jedidiah responded, "I'm sure that must have been regrettable to have heard your father say that."

"It did at first, but that's how he has always been toward me. He never liked me. I heard him say he resents that I was born. My mom is the only one who ever loved me." His eyes filled with tears as he remembered his mother, her death, and all the anger his father showed him.

"Why do you think your mother loved you so much?"

Wiping his eyes, "She was my mom. I guess that was her job."

"So, you figured out that it was her *job* to love you?"

"Well, yeah, that's what moms are supposed to do."

"It wasn't her job, Jonathan. Your mother loved you because you were part of her. You were a special gift, and she realized how precious and *unique* you are. All this time, you've had it all wrong, my young friend; you don't have to do something special to be someone special. Understand something: you don't have to prove anything to anyone. The only person you need to prove anything to is yourself.

I seem to remember someone saying that very same thing to me not long ago. Jonathan thought.

"You are in the process of finding the real treasure and don't even realize it. Jonathan, you are one of a kind. No one on this earth is just like you. And you should be proud of who you are!"

"Yeah, a *loser!*"

"You aren't a loser. That's not who you *really* are. I think you know that but don't want to believe it's true because you've heard it for years. Look here, hold out your hands like a cup." Jonathan held out his hands, cupped palms up. Jedidiah reached down and scooped up sand in his hands. He held his hands above Jonathan's and let the sand slowly slip through his fists in a gentle but steady stream into Jonathan's. "Our lives are like this sand, Jonathan. The sand in an hourglass. Each grain of sand is like a single day of our lives. Once the sand passes through the narrow gap in the glass, it is gone—it is past. All we have is the sand that remains at the top; we never know how much sand we have left. There's a saying from the ancient Greek philosopher, Socrates, that goes something like this: 'Our lives are but specks of dust falling through the fingers of time. Like sands of the hourglass, so are the days of our lives.' The only moment you have any control over is the moment you sit in right here, right now! The past is gone; you can't do anything about it, and the future is yours to make. Listen, Jonathan, you need to understand something else. What your reality reflects to you is always what you are carrying inside you right here, right now. You should think long and hard about that. Start enjoying the time you have and make the most of it! You are an extraordinary person—one of a kind! There is no one else like you on the face of the earth, and there never will be." Looking down at his hands, Jonathan let the sand fall from them.

Jedidiah dusted off his hands as Jonathan sat there motionless. "Look at the past few weeks. Isn't that proof enough for you? You've done an incredible job here and were instrumental in making a significant archaeological discovery! Your instincts took you to a place none of the rest of us thought to look! *You* figured it out! *You* took a chance! *You* made the discovery!" Jedidiah tried to convince Jonathan of what he said. "Have you ever considered trying to love yourself?"

Jonathan was confused. "Huh?"

"What I mean is: appreciate yourself and who you are as a person."

He paused for a moment. "What do you mean, *try to appreciate who I am as a person*? No, I've hated myself. I'm nothing, a nobody, a screw-up." He threw up his arms in exasperation, "What is there to appreciate? I've never done anything important!"

"Why are you saying that? Because that's what your father told you for years? Or do you truly believe those things about yourself? You've already told me your father said those things out of anger and resentment. Can you consider you are worthy of love, that it isn't someone's *job* to love you, and that you *deserve* love? And most importantly, the first person who needs to love and appreciate you *is you*!"

Jonathan sat absentmindedly, poking at the fire with a stick. He wanted to believe what Jedidiah said but had difficulty accepting it himself. "Can you consider that? Will you consider that Kate sees something in you worthy of loving and apparently, she always has?"

"I don't know. I just don't know. My life is so conflicted right now."

"I am just asking; can you consider it? Kate's feelings for you seem strange to you now because you don't consider yourself worthy of someone else's love, let alone your own. Just think about it."

He considered what Jedidiah had said. Jedidiah saw the faintest glimmer that Jonathan understood what he meant, then it was gone, and doubt reappeared. Jedidiah got up and put his hand on Jonathan's shoulder. "Just consider what I have said. Consider the possibility that you deserve much more than only recognition." Then, he walked away.

Jonathan was puzzled by Jedidiah's last statement and turned. "Wait, Jed . . ." but Jedidiah had disappeared into the night.

He decided to keep himself at an emotional distance from Kate and Mark. Kate's declaration made him uncomfortable, and Mark's apparent awareness of those feelings bothered him. He spent a restless night mulling over everything. Sleeping was impossible, so once again, he wrote.

Love myself. Appreciate myself? What the heck does that mean? I deserve more than recognition? What's more important than being someone important—someone famous, someone who has accomplished something special? And love—what is all that about? Kate in love with me, really? All I've ever known is anger and frustration. I wonder why my parents stayed together with all the yelling that went on around the house. My father's wrath and the tension we lived with every day was almost unbearable at times. But it was me—I made their lives miserable. I'm not dumb. I know they had to get married because of me. I've always been a mistake. It's better I keep my interactions with Mark and Kate to a minimum for a while. I have got to try and figure this all out.

THE TRUE DISCOVERY

The next day, Jonathan, Mark, and Kate worked on cataloging other items from the dig. Jonathan kept the conversation very business-like. "Mark, do you have the sherds from grid thirty-five all cataloged?"

"Yep, they are all cataloged, packed up, and ready to go."

"How about the ones we collected during the storage room excavation? I'm certain Jedidiah will be particularly interested in them. They may help date the time of the earthquake."

"Yes, they are all done as well."

Jonathan did not want to talk about what happened between them, but Kate did. She seemed to open her mouth to speak but looked away and never spoke. He saw her looking at him from time to time. Alas, during work, she never mentioned anything, which Jonathan appreciated.

Later, Jonathan sat eating by himself in the cook shack, and Kate came over and sat with him. She started to talk, but Jonathan cut her short. "I don't want to talk about it right now."

She frowned and got up and left the table without saying another word.

Mark saw what happened and got up from the table where he had been sitting with other team members and went over to Jonathan. Before he could even sit down, Jonathan blurted out, "I don't want to talk about it!"

"Talk about what—your disappointment in not finding gold and jewels or your attitude toward Kate and me? You need to talk to someone."

"Frankly, I wish I had never come on this stupid trip!"

"And why's that?" Mark leaned over the table almost in Jonathan's face. "Are you out of your comfort zone? Out of playing the victim and wallowing in self-pity as you've done for years back home? What is it? As your best friend, I'd like to know!"

Jonathan stood and slammed his fists on the table. The dishes rattled, so everyone turned. All the eyes on Jonathan shook him. *Wow, Mark is right.* He sat and calmed down. "I'm sorry, Mark." It occurred to him that Mark had been right about a lot of things. But Jonathan hadn't wanted to talk about those things, even with his best friend.

Mark continued, "I've known you the better part of my life and consider you to be my best friend. Why is it that you find it so difficult to talk to me? I've shared some of my most difficult times with you; you've always listened as a friend. Though your father mistreated you and made your life a living hell, that's in the past. You're done with him now. You need to let it go. Stop wearing your father's anger and resentment like some badge of courage! You can't continue to give him power over your life, and you don't have to deal with him anymore. You're better than that—*more than that*! I talked you into coming on this adventure, and it *has been* an *amazing* adventure to start a new page in your life and write a new story of yourself. Start living the life your mom believed you could have. You have a shot at that, Jon. Don't kick someone to the ground who's loved you for most of her life."

Jonathan stared at his food. In less than twenty-four hours, three people gave him things to think about—uncomfortable things to think about. Mark left Jonathan sitting alone.

Jonathan found it too complicated and confusing to consider there could be another way to live—he'd only known pain and anger his whole life. Unfortunately, disappointment and hatred seemed to overshadow the little bit of love and encouragement he did receive from his mother. And continued to plague him on this expedition.

Mark made it sound so simple to change. Sure, I get what he's saying, and he's probably right, but I can't snap my fingers and change. I can't deal with this, plus the shock that Kate has been in love with me for years.

Jonathan left the cook shack and wandered his way to the dig site to finish cataloging their most recent finds. Soon, Mark's words continued to overturn in his mind and interrupted his concentration on the work at hand. He left the site and walked out to the ledge overlooking the desert that had become his thinking place. He retrieved his journal from his backpack and jotted down a few thoughts.

> *I still don't understand Kate's profession of love. How could I have not picked up on her feelings? I never thought anyone would ever want to be with a loser like me. It never seemed in the realm of possibility, especially Kate. What does she see in me?*

He left the ledge and its solitude, and after wandering a bit more, Jonathan looked for Reverend Ken because he wanted to talk through the things bothering him, especially Kate and her feelings. It felt unusual because Jonathan never sought spiritual counseling because he felt religion was pretty hypocritical—go to church on Sunday and then treat people like crap the other six days of the week. But after getting to know Reverend Ken better, Jonathan sought his input, particularly regarding this matter.

Jonathan found Reverend Ken in his tent. "Good evening, Reverend Ken. May I speak with you for a few minutes?"

"Sure, please come in and have a seat. What's on your mind?"

"Well, I'm a bit confused over several things in the past couple of days. I'd like to talk to you about them if you have the time."

"Of course, what's going on with you? I know you are disappointed our discovery wasn't monetary gold and such, but the discovery was crucial for our mission."

"I understand about that, sir. Part of this is personal and close to home."

Reverend Ken lifted an eyebrow. "What is it, Jonathan?"

"Um, the other day, Kate told me she has loved me since sixth grade."

Reverend Ken smiled. "Yes, I've surmised that for a while now."

"Has she talked to you about it?"

"Well, not in so many words, but she *is* my daughter and does confide in me about important things. That's always been the relationship she and I have had."

Jonathan was surprised because he could never speak with either of his parents about his feelings or problems. He never attempted to talk with his father because *kids should be seen and not heard*.

An old memory flashed into Jonathan's mind when he visited his grandparents with his father; he had to *sit on the couch and be quiet while the grown-ups talked*. He and his parents gained the house after his grandfather died. A funny thing was that that particular couch still sat in the same spot in the living room. It had faded on one arm over the years where the sun came in through the window. *Why didn't they get rid of that old couch when we moved into the house?* As if it was yesterday, he pictured his grandfather sitting at the dining table. "Kids are to be seen and not heard, and don't touch anything." Jonathan could almost hear his father say that as though he was in the room. Jonathan learned very quickly to keep his thoughts and feelings to himself or possibly get backhanded across the face. When he tried to tell his mother something, she would say, "That's nice, dear," patted him on the head, and walked away. She was always too busy.

Jonathan returned from his memories as Reverend Ken continued, "Ah, so, what's the problem?"

"Well, she said she has loved me since sixth grade; it took me by surprise. Kate and I have been friends for years, but I never thought of her romantically. I've never thought of *anyone* in that way." It was hard for Jonathan to continue.

"Why do you think that is, Jonathan?" Reverend Ken asked.

THE TRUE DISCOVERY

"The other night, I was talking to Jedidiah about this, and he said something about loving myself, which sounded totally weird and egotistical to me."

"It's not weird or egotistical. Every human being has a little bit of God—or whatever you want to call the elemental energy of everything in creation—in them. We all are special in some unique way. You look at God in the mirror."

"That's kinda what Jedidiah said."

"I think Jedidiah meant you need to realize what makes you special. Though you didn't have the best of circumstances growing up, you *are* worthy of love, and my daughter is sensitive enough to know that, and she loves you."

"How exactly do I learn to love myself, Reverend Ken?"

"Well, first of all, there isn't an exact way to love yourself. The first thing is to try to let go of your past and let go of your father's anger and resentment. Your birth was a magical and exceptional event. You need to believe that with all your heart. Whatever your father had—or has—going on is his problem, not yours."

"I'm so confused."

"You can't start living in the present until you let go of what went on in the past. Yes, it happened, but you don't need to allow it to continue to control and dominate your life and your present happiness. You know something, Jonathan, most people back up into their future, dragging the past with them. Many people, like you, keep reliving old hurts and pain, which prevents them from enjoying and taking pleasure in what's happening right now—the excitement of the present moment."

"Yes, but how do I stop letting my past keep following me like a dark shadow?"

"I'm not saying it's easy to do or can happen overnight, but you *do* have people who care about you and love you. Loving yourself comes with a little practice and paying attention to your thoughts and feelings."

"But most of the time, I think negative thoughts about myself and everything around me. *Bad thoughts!*"

Reverend Hogan leaned in close to make sure Jonathan understood, "Over the years, you've learned to push down or dismiss any good thoughts or feelings. You're in reaction mode all of the time rather than controlling what you can. In your mind, you conditioned yourself to always view situations, people, and even *you* as negative or *bad*. This is *not* true! You can always control your emotions and how you react. When things don't go how you want, you complain, blame other people or conditions, and run away rather than taking responsibility. Look at what's happened in the past few days. You were instrumental in discovering one of the most important archaeological finds since the Dead Sea Scrolls. You saw what none of the rest of us were able to see. Instead of excitement, you threw a tantrum because it wasn't what *you* wanted it to be.

"I know, that was really bad."

"Now, you've found out someone special loves you. And instead of being happy, you turned and ran, rejecting the thought. I'd say those were two pretty important things, and you let baggage from your past mess both of them up."

Listen, there is a little story I'd like you to hear. It's called *Acres of Diamonds*. It's not my story; it came from Russell Conwell, the founder of Temple University.

He told the story in one of his lectures. It goes something like this: A farmer in Africa heard from his neighbors that they were finding diamonds on their land, so the farmer started looking for diamonds on his land. When he didn't find any, he sold it and searched far and wide for diamonds and riches. Years passed, and he never found any. In despair, he threw himself in a river and drowned. Well, the farmer who bought the land was wise and knew what raw diamonds looked like, and one day in a stream that flowed on the land, he found a large raw diamond. The farmer's land became one of the richest diamond mines in Africa, and the farmer who

THE TRUE DISCOVERY

bought the land was rich beyond measure. Jonathan, you need to recognize that you are a diamond. You have accomplished so much here. You need to realize what you have within and stop searching outside yourself for something of value.

Jonathan sat there momentarily with a confused look on his face. "Thanks, Reverend Ken. You've given me a lot to think about. I think I am going to call it a night."

"Good evening, Jonathan. I hope our conversation helped." Jonathan left, hung his head, stuffed his hands in his pockets, and felt more conflicted than before.

He did not call it a night; instead, he once again went out to the ledge overlooking the desert where he seemed to have found a place of refuge and peace. Trying to sort through his thoughts, he began to write.

> *I don't understand what is going on inside my head. My life seemed so simple before—miserable and screwed up—but simple. But now I'm valuable, relevant, and worthy of love—just because? They all said I need to learn to love myself. I don't have to prove I'm special to anyone, and there is someone in my life who has loved me for years, but I never realized it.*
>
> *But haven't I been a loser my whole life because I haven't accomplished anything important, ever? I mean, instead of finding a treasure room, I discovered a king's old pottery. Sure, maybe some guy stuck in the back of a museum or university will find it valuable. But all the real glory goes to Jedidiah and Reverend Ken because this is their dig. Things are so messed up!*

He packed up the journal and returned to his tent, but he continued degrading himself. *As usual, once again, Jonathan Tobias is a loser, second fiddle—a might have been! It's not right; it's not fair. I found the staircase leading to the room!*

He grumbled, "All this talk about intrinsic value and looking within is a bunch of hogwash. The only way to make people know you are important is to do something special! I wish I had found some diamonds!"

FIFTEEN

REVELATION

The following day after breakfast, Jonathan headed toward the research tent to finish up some cataloging when he saw Kate. She eyed him and approached him. He rolled his eyes as she approached. *I might as well get this over with.*

Kate was happy and smiling. "Hey, my dad told me you stopped by and talked with him last night. How'd it go?"

"Lousy, if you really need to know."

Her mood instantly changed. "What's wrong now?" She stamped her foot, exasperated.

"Oh, nothing, or *everything*! I can't deal with my life or you right now!"

"I don't know what's the matter with you, *you stupid lousy jerk*!" Kate choked back tears. Everyone who cares about you has gone out of their way to be helpful, kind, supportive, and generous to you for years and years, and you've been too stupid, brooding, moody, and blind to realize or even care! You hate your life; I get it. And conveniently, you blame your father for all your problems. Well, the real problem is *you*!" She pushed him in frustration.

"Hold on a minute!"

"No! Your mother couldn't even get the idea of your worth through your thick skull!"

"You leave my mother out of this; you didn't know anything about her!"

"I know enough about love, and I'm talking about *you*!" She shoved him, and he lost his footing. "I don't know why I've wasted all these years loving you. You wouldn't know what love is if I hit you over the head with it! You're *hopeless* and *clueless*!" With that, Kate stormed off, crying.

Jonathan froze in place. He opened his mouth to say something but instead watched her run away. He wandered through the dig site and thought about what Jedidiah, Reverend Ken, Mark, and Kate had said and ended up at the top of the staircase leading to the now empty room. Jonathan sat down on the first stone that started it all. *I wish I'd never uncovered this rock! My life feels like that dark empty hole down there in the ground!* It had only been a few days, but it felt like a lifetime with all this upheaval. He rested his elbows on his knees, rubbed his head in dismay, and berated himself for being so harsh with Kate. *None of this is her fault. I overreacted again, like that night in the Southend Café when she and Mark were only trying to help me with my finances, and I lost my temper with her.* "I'm such a jerk!"

Jonathan stood and slowly walked down the steps and entered the room. He realized it was the first time he'd returned to the place since the discovery because being there reminded him of his disappointment and embarrassment. Jonathan noticed the bare walls in the faint light from the open doorway. "They've even removed the door. This place *is* just like my life—*empty*." The hollow sound of his voice echoed back to him.

The chamber felt like a carcass picked over by a flock of vultures. At that moment, a slight tremor immediately followed by a much stronger shockwave knocked Jonathan to the floor. The walls above the room entrance collapsed with a loud crash, filling the staircase with stone, rubble, and dust.

Jonathan hit his head in the fall. Stunned and dazed, he only saw total darkness. Something ran down his face, and he

REVELATION

realized he had a cut on his head, but everything else seemed alright. Trapped all alone in the darkness, he breathed heavy and coughed a few times from the dust. *No one knows I'm down here. We removed all the things we found, so there isn't anything important down here, not even me.* He could almost hear his dad, hands on his hips, saying, "Yep, look what you got yourself into."

"Help! Help me; I'm down here!"

After a few more deep breaths, he realized no one could possibly hear him because the rubble was too deep to allow any noise through. *What else could go wrong and happen to me now? Once again, wrong place, wrong time.* Suddenly, he thought about Kate, Mark, Reverend Ken, Jedidiah, and all the others. I hope they are okay!"

He opened and closed his eyes several times and rubbed his head, trying desperately to focus and make sense of his situation. Sitting up, he reached around him, trying to determine if he was near one of the walls. Confused and disoriented, he wondered what happened? *It must have been another earthquake.*

Taking out his handkerchief, he dabbed at the blood running down his face. *Yuck. It's not too painful, and I don't feel a lot of blood. I think I'm okay. Besides, this cut is the least of my worries right now.* He scraped his palms and knees as he crawled across the debris-strewn floor until he reached what he thought was the far wall of the room. Scooting against it, he pulled his knees to his chest, dusted off his hands, and dabbed at the blood and sweat on his forehead with his soiled handkerchief. *How long would it take them to find me, even if they knew where to look? Oh no, will I die of asphyxiation?* Jonathan momentarily tensed. He started to hyperventilate but remembered he should conserve his oxygen. Soon, he calmed down and resigned himself to wait and see if someone came to his rescue before he suffocated.

The moments ticked on. In the cold darkness, he wondered if this would ultimately be his tomb. *How fittingly ironic.*

He had nothing but time to think about everything. And despite all he'd known—anger, harsh words, disappointment, a messed-up family, self-blame—he realized he had made others' lives miserable with *his* attitude. *Wow! My big reveal! How screwed up is that?*

Jonathan reflected on his mom's love. She had tried her best to make him feel like he was okay—maybe a little different—but that was alright. He remembered when his father told his mother he was sorry Jonathan was born. *Our lives would have been so different without him, so much better!* His father's words echoed in Jonathan's head all these years later. But honestly, others teased him at school, too, even the teachers, so he always felt like an outcast or oddball. *It never occurred to anyone that I might have had a learning disability. They labeled me as a lousy student, a bad kid, and those labels followed me until I dropped out of high school.* But when he and Mark met and became friends in first grade, those were Jonathan's first fond memories. *Gosh, those were great times. We had so much fun playing make-believe and creating adventures. I forgot how much fun we had and what it meant to have a good friend.*

Jonathan's mind went to Mark's parents and how different they were from Pete and Mary Ann. *It felt like they loved me as much as they loved him. Man, staying overnight at their house was the best because Mrs. Atkins made sure I had plenty to eat. And Mr. Atkins was always interested in my day.* It occurred to Jonathan that he may have envied Mark a little bit back then—and now—because his parents were so kind. *I felt cheated because my parents weren't anything like his.* It seemed strange he had forgotten about those times and how Mark's parents made him feel *special*. They made him feel *loved*. *Wow, I focused on the negative things and forgot all the good stuff. I wonder if other people do that. Why is it so easy to pay so much attention to the negative things and forget the good things?*

His friendship with Mark brought him to his relationship with Kate. *I forgot how she became a part of our friendship and*

REVELATION

seemed a natural part of our childhood threesome. He chuckled when he thought of her as a tomboy with pigtails and jeans. *She hated being the damsel in distress when we played pirates or knights.* How strange and far away that seemed in the dark. He smiled, remembering the joy of their childhood together.

As soon as he smiled, he remembered Kate's declaration of romantic love for him and felt his stomach drop. It stunned him because he never considered himself loveable, but he also felt like such an unworthy screwup. *I always figured Kate would end up with Mark. He was the handsome, athletic type, the perfect cliche of the all-American male. I wonder what it is about me that attracted her. Maybe I should have asked her before acting like a jerk!*

Jonathan's thoughts circled back to the past few days. He recognized that his jealousy, pain, and anger overwhelmed him because it's all he ever knew and wanted. *Mark was right. I've worn my victimhood like a badge of honor, wallowing in it, and what has the selfishness gotten me? Nothing, absolutely nothing! I decided if I found wealth, then I'd be famous and someone special. But instead, we found Solomon's riches, knowledge of his existence, artifacts more valuable than gold and jewels could ever be.* "What a stupid, stupid fool I've been!" He eased himself up the wall and moved along it, feeling his way in the darkness until he found the rubble strewn on the floor, blocking the door. Defeated, he sat down again on one of the larger stones.

As the minutes ticked on, Jedidiah's compassionate words brought revelation to Jonathan's spirit. Jedidiah told him his mother loved him so much because she knew he was special, unique, and one of a kind; no one else was quite like him. That made him unique. "I guess in pursuit of inadvertently proving my dad right, I thought special constituted doing something special, and not simply the fact being who God made me was enough." Jonathan thumped himself on the forehead with the palm of his hand. "I came searching for something valuable, something to make me special, not realizing my specialness was always inside of me! That diamond Reverend Ken talked about."

What a waste of time wallowing in my self-pity and anger. *Jedidiah was right; I've been so blind not to realize someone doesn't have to be famous to be special. I would rather be me than anyone else in the world!* Jonathan cradled his head in his hands in disbelief at what a mess he made of his life. Finally, he realized when friends care, love, and depend on you, you *are* special. And when you touch other lives in good, positive ways, give more than you take, share, live in the moment, relish every second, and practice gratitude for everything that comes your way, you *are* special. *I've let others down because I spent my life pitying myself.*

Most importantly, I let myself down. How on earth could I make up for all the trouble I caused and apologize to Mark and Kate for acting like a child? I've blamed circumstances when I've been at fault all along. And now I've alienated my two best friends—my only friends.

As he contemplated, it took his mind away from his current situation for a while. After a short time, his thoughts returned to his physical location and his situation. He pondered what was happening outside. *How long has it been? I hope there weren't any other injuries in the quake. It had to have been an earthquake.* He felt drunk. *Mom ironed on Tuesdays, but Monday was laundry day, so why did she iron on Tuesdays, and why did she iron everything, even our underwear and socks? Did other women iron socks?* Jonathan shook his head. *What? Where did that come from? Why am I thinking about socks?* The fuzziness enveloped him, and he couldn't seem to think straight. *I wish Mark and Kate were here; they would know what to do.* An almost euphoric state overtook him, then . . . blackness.

SIXTEEN

RECONCILIATION

The darkness slowly dissipated. Jonathan gradually opened his eyes, and somewhere in the back of his mind, he remembered the earthquake and his entrapment in the underground room. As his vision cleared, Jonathan found himself in another strange place. It was some magnificent hall with ornately placed decorations and lavish centerpieces. The vast room had two rows of columns on either side, at least thirty feet high. The lower parts of the columns were fluted and covered in gold. In contrast, the columns' upper parts were smooth, a deep red colored stone with magnificent capitals carved with bulls' heads facing opposite directions that supported a roof of carved timbers inlaid with gold.

Crowds of people stood near the columns. There was a sunken, vast area in the center of the room. The people near the columns looked down on the scene in the center of the room. A staircase rose to a golden throne at the far end, an ornate chair with golden lions created the armrests. Fourteen life-size gold lions led up the stairs, seven on each side. A beautiful carpet of many colors covered the center of the stone stairs. There were two columns of gold and ivory on either side of the throne. A group of beautifully dressed women stood to the right and behind the throne, and musicians sat below. He saw some tables full of different kinds of food; elegant draperies hung behind the throne, and two live peacocks stood near the staircase. It must have been an elaborate ceremony. A beautiful, exotic woman stood on the steps, followed by many servants carrying chests filled with gold, jewels, aromatic spices, and beautiful fabrics as gifts for this king. The king sat on the throne, partially obscured by draperies hanging from the columns. Scents of incense seemed to fill the air. The musicians were poised to play music. A group of men who appeared to be important stood to the left of the great throne. The whole scene was like something from an old big-budget Biblical movie. It was a spectacular room from another time and place.

Where the heck am I? What is this place, and how did I get here? Is this a dream? It must be a dream! Am I dead? He stood in the crowd of people. Everyone wore flowing robes, and the men wore many different hats, turbans, or scarves. The women wore jewels and scarves of many colors. He yelled, "Where *am* I?" No one in the room noticed his frantic scream. Jonathan realized everyone and everything in this spectacular scene appeared frozen in time. He felt like he was standing inside a three-dimensional painting; no one was even aware of his presence.

He shook his head from side to side and rubbed his eyes. *Am I seeing things? What is happening to me? This isn't real, but somehow it feels real. What is going on? Is this King Solomon's throne room? Why am I here? I must be dead!* He panicked for a moment. The king leaned forward to speak, but Jonathan couldn't comprehend what he saw because the man on the throne looked exactly like Jedidiah! *What the heck?* The man was younger with a fuller, dark beard, and he had long dark hair beneath the golden crown, but there was no mistake; the king *was* Jedidiah sitting on the throne. He held that same benevolent countenance he had experienced so often during the past few weeks. He knew that same feeling of calmness

RECONCILIATION

and soul searching he felt the first time he met Jedidiah. There was no doubt in his mind who this king was!

Everyone remained frozen but the king. He looked over and saw Jonathan standing in the crowd. He descended the steps before the throne and walked directly toward Jonathan. *It was Jedidiah Cohen!* The king smiled at him, reached out, and placed his right hand on Jonathan's shoulder.

"Are you King Solomon?"

"Yes, my young friend. That is one of my names."

He waved his left arm in a gesture to acknowledge the scene before them. Then, Solomon spoke, "You, Jonathan Tobias, came to this place seeking riches and glory. But my young friend, you have found much, much more than gold and jewels. You have found true wealth—wisdom. The wealth you always possessed—your specialness, the treasure you have always carried within, self-love. You have realized what true friendship is, what service to others means, and the love of another person." In that instant, Jonathan experienced the overwhelming sense of peace and tranquility within him, which he had known before in Jedidiah's presence.

Then, way off in the distance, he heard his mother's voice calling him, "Jonathan, Jonathan!" His head spun, and as the fog in his head cleared, he realized it wasn't his mother's voice, but it was Kate's voice. *She hasn't called me Jonathan in years.* He felt the hand on his shoulder, and the vision dissolved.

"Jonathan, Jonathan, can you hear me? You're safe now."

He struggled to open his eyes, and when he did, he found himself in a hospital room and saw Kate on the edge of his bed.

"What happened? Where am I?"

Kate replied, "You're in Hadassah Ein Kerem Hospital in Jerusalem. They brought you here after we dug you out of that awful underground room. You almost died!"

"Yeah, we all thought you were a goner, buddy," Mark replied from the other side of the room.

"How did you know I was down there?"

"We took a headcount after the quake. When we realized the walls had collapsed, Jedidiah suggested we look for you down there." She pointed to Jedidiah, who was also in the hospital room.

"Is everyone else okay? Did anyone else get hurt in the quake?"

Reverend Ken walked over to his bed. "No, fortunately, no one else was severely injured. There were some scrapes and bruises from falls but nothing serious, thank goodness!"

"What about the specimens and your research, Reverend Ken?"

"No, everything is fine. Only concern yourself with getting better. The hospital is going to keep you here for a couple of days for observation. You received a minor head injury; it was a pretty close call, young man. You were in the first stages of anoxia when we found you. A few minutes later, you would have been dead."

Jedidiah was standing at the foot of his bed. He smiled the same mysterious smile Jonathan remembered from the vision.

"I am glad to see that you are well, Jonathan Tobias," Jedidiah said, patting Jonathan's foot. With that, he started to leave the room but turned briefly with his hand on the door and said, "You'll be *just fine* now, my young friend." He nodded his head and, with a smile, winked and disappeared, closing the door behind him.

Later that day, Jonathan stayed in his hospital bed after everyone left. He felt tired but found it difficult to relax and doze off. The nurses came in and checked his vital signs and changed his IV. *They sure didn't stay very long. I thought they would have some news and want to chat a bit.* Once again, he felt alone with his thoughts. It occurred to him that perhaps writing

RECONCILIATION

them down could help him make more sense of things. He rang the nurse to ask, "Did they happen to bring a backpack that I had with me when they brought me to the hospital?"

"I don't know for sure, but I'll check."

A few minutes later, she returned with his battered backpack in hand.

"I believe this is it?"

"Yes, it is. Thank you very much."

Within, he found his well-used journal and began to write. He recounted everything that had happened.

> *Mark and Kate were right. I spent the most significant part of my life playing the victim role, blaming other people, circumstances, and life for all my problems when it had always been me, my bitterness, and self-pity.*
>
> *My thoughts, negative attitude, and actions were the source of everything wrong in my life. My self-pity and blame blinded me, making me a prisoner in my self-imposed miserable life. Now that I can think more clearly, I know what I need to do now and what I have to change if I expect my life to improve. Unfortunately, it took almost dying to make me realize I am a unique person.*

He sat up in the bed and unraveled the sheet that had tangled underneath him with his tossing and turning. He continued.

> *I have unique skills, talents, and abilities. And I proved it to myself and everyone who mattered. I need to continue to share what I learned here—living in the moment and practicing gratitude for the good and the bad because, without the bad, I can't ever cherish the good.*

Jonathan pondered his thoughts before writing more. Then, he continued.

It sets us up for a life well-lived when we surround ourselves with reciprocal nurturing and supportive friends and relationships. Also, when you love yourself, you're capable of accepting love and receiving love in return.

I understand the past is the past. Though I can't change it, I can stop wallowing in it and allowing all of my father's anger and resentment to control my present.

Finally, after serious contemplation, he was exhausted and drifted off to sleep.

On his last morning in the hospital, Jonathan woke, excited to leave. But it felt strange that no one had come to visit him since just after he regained consciousness. *Does everyone hate me now?* When he signed all the necessary paperwork to leave, it was a relief when Reverend Hogan came to pick him up.

They left the hospital and started the trip back to the dig site.

"Reverend Ken, where are Kate and Mark? Why didn't anyone come to visit while I was in the hospital?" Jonathan asked.

"They're busy back at the dig site."

"I thought they might have come to visit with me or at least come along with you to pick me up."

"Well, to be honest, I don't think they are quite ready to forgive you yet for your recent behavior, particularly Kate." Jonathan felt sick to realize his worst fears.

"I don't understand. They were at the hospital the other day, and everything seemed fine."

RECONCILIATION

"They were glad to find out you were okay and out of danger. That doesn't mean Mark and Kate have forgiven you *yet* for the way you've treated them."

"Oh, but I'm not the same person as before! I realized how terrible I was and the mistakes I've made!"

Reverend Hogan pulled the jeep to the side of the road, stopped, and placed his hand on Jonathan's shoulder and looked directly into Jonathan's eyes. "I'm afraid you're going to have to prove it to them, and in terms of Kate, that might be a *real* challenge. You've managed to break her heart, my young friend. I'm sorry to tell you this, Jonathan, but I'm afraid it's a fact you're going to have to rectify." He then pulled back onto the road and continued to the dig site.

As they traveled, Jonathan pondered how to restore what he destroyed. He reached down and pulled his journal from the backpack between his legs. Though the road was bumpy, he wanted to journal his thoughts and grabbed the pen he'd shoved inside the front and placed the journal on his lap.

"What's that you have there?" Reverend Hogan asked.

"Oh, it's my journal. I keep it with me all of the time. It helps me if I write my thoughts down. As I said, I'm not the same person. Writing helps me to sort through my behavior and thoughts, and hopefully, I can figure out how to make amends with Mark and Kate," Jonathan said matter-of-factly.

Reverend Hogan smiled. "Now that is a great idea, Jonathan. You have my prayers to find a peaceful resolution."

Jonathan wrote down his thoughts.

How am I going to be able to show Mark and Kate I'm different now? How can I say I'm genuinely sorry? How can I make amends with them? Will I be able to repair these most important relationships? Things can't go back to the way they were before; I'm not that person anymore. We still have two weeks at the dig site, and there is still a lot to finalize before returning home. Maybe I still have a chance.

They arrived at the dig site. Jonathan returned the journal to his backpack and slung it over his shoulder as he got out of the jeep, "Thank you for picking me up. I appreciate your kindness."

"You're welcome, Jonathan. I think Mark and Kate are working on grid thirty-two, finalizing things. You'll probably find them there."

"Thanks again for everything, Reverend Ken."

"You're welcome, Jonathan. And the three of you are in my thoughts and prayers."

Jonathan walked over to grid thirty-two, where he saw Kate and Mark working and went to say hello to his two friends.

When he approached, he felt shy. Sheepishly, Jonathan said, "Hey, guys. How's it going? Had any luck finding anything interesting today?"

Mark looked up. "Hi, Jon. Glad you're back." Kate looked up at him briefly with a sad and hurt expression that tore Jonathan's heart out, but he did not say anything.

They returned to their work, digging and sifting through the dirt and sand.

Jonathan said, "Looks pretty much like life as usual at the dig. Shovel and sift, shovel and sift." He smiled an awkward smile, sensed the chill in the air at his attempt to be funny, and decided to leave things without pushing for more. "Thank you both for helping to rescue me from the room and for coming to the hospital to see me. I really appreciate your concern for me and our friendship." When neither Mark nor Kate responded, he said, "Well, I better go and check in and see if there is anything I can do to help with on the dig."

With that, he walked off. Mark poked Kate and asked, "Why didn't you even say hello to him?"

"Because I'm not ready to say hello—or anything else—to him right now. I'm glad he didn't die trapped in that *stupid* room, but I'm not ready to speak to him yet. He's still a jerk, as far as I'm concerned."

RECONCILIATION

In the meantime, Jonathan looked around the dig site. Once again, he found himself standing at the staircase to the room. They had removed the rubble from the fallen walls and piled it to the side. Jonathan sat on the top step on the same block of stone that began his real journey. *To think I almost died down there in that hole in the ground. If it hadn't been for Jedidiah, I probably would have. I know it was him in my vision, and I know I didn't imagine the whole thing, but how did he know I was trapped down there?* He looked down into the darkness of the empty room. *The old Jonathan died down there. Now, how is the new, living Jonathan going to make amends? I've done things, hurt others, and wasted years of love and friendship. How do I say I'm sorry? How will I prove to Mark and Kate I am not the idiot I was before—I'm not that jerk. How can I show them how much I value and appreciate their friendship?* He rested his elbows on his knees and covered his face with his hands. "Please, God, show me the way! I am so sorry for what I've done, for how I've treated my best friends and others in my life!"

∞

At that same time, Kate and Mark continued talking about Jonathan's feeble attempt to try to resolve his issues with each of them.

"I don't know if he learned a single thing, and I certainly don't want to sit there and listen to him bemoan his *bad luck* at being trapped in that room and almost dying! *Oh, poor me. Just my luck! I almost died!*" Kate put her hand on her forehead and pretended to faint.

"I think you are making more of it than you should. The whole situation was pretty traumatic and got Jon thinking."

"Well, I don't think I can stand to hear one more word out of his mouth. He has been such a hateful jerk! I don't know why I still care so much for him after everything that's happened. It's hard for me to forget and forgive the way he treated us. He's not the person I thought he was."

"He did try to start a conversation a few minutes ago, though."

"It'll take a whole lot more than a feeble hello and thank you from him for me to believe he has changed." She jabbed at the ground with her trowel. "Why did I waste so much time thinking he would change as we grew up? Why didn't he notice I never dated anyone through high school and even later? He is so self-centered and didn't even realize I wanted him all along!" She began to cry.

"It'll be okay." Mark hugged her once again.

She wiped a tear from her eye. "No, I don't think it will ever be the same for me."

But Mark sensed a change in Jonathan and continued to defend him. "I don't think he realized what his constant griping and complaining sounded like and how he dragged everyone around him down. He was clueless. There are all kinds of people like Jon, oblivious like him." Mark shrugged his shoulders.

"Yeah, I'll give him that—he *is* clueless and oblivious about everyone but himself."

"You know he wasn't that way when we were kids. I first noticed it when we became teenagers—his complaining started and got worse over the past couple of years."

Kate replied, "Hey, I get it. He had a terrible life at home, but I don't think that is any excuse for being so horrible to us, particularly now when we're trying to help. I think he's been worse than ever on this trip. One minute he seems fine but the next, he's acting like a spoiled child! I never know what to think or what to say around him!"

Mark still dug and sifted through the dirt. "I thought having him come on this trip, getting away from home, dealing with his mother's death, and his father kicking him out of the house would help him try to move on with his life. I don't know; maybe it wasn't such a good idea. And his disappointment in not finding buried treasure made things even worse." He shook his head in regret.

"By the way, where *did* he get the idea that we were coming on this dig to look for treasure anyway?" she asked.

Mark held up his hands in defense. "Honest, I swear! I never said *anything* about treasure when we talked about coming. I don't know how Jon got that idea in his head."

She knocked the dust off her hands and removing her gloves as she stood. "Well, we aren't going to be able to continue to give him the cold shoulder for the rest of this trip. We'll need to talk to him again, but I'm not looking forward to the conversation," Kate replied.

Another day passed, and the friends only exchanged pleasantries. Jonathan thought he would go crazy without his friends, but he didn't know how to start the conversation. Once again, he went to Reverend Ken and asked if he had seen Jedidiah.

"I'm sorry, but Jedidiah completed his work here at the dig. He was in charge of documenting the items from the storage room for the Israeli government. I doubt we'll see him again before we leave."

Jonathan said to him, "Then, can I speak to you about all that has happened and ask your advice?"

"Sure, Jonathan, I am all ears."

"Well, sir, I know I have been a total jerk for a long time, but I am not the same person anymore."

"You told me that on the way back from the hospital, and I believe I told you at the time that actions speak louder than words."

"That's my problem. I don't know what to do or say to show Mark and Kate I've changed. How do I demonstrate to my two best friends that I'm not a jerk anymore? Especially Kate!"

"The first step is to recognize your past behavior. By the way, you aren't a jerk. You might have been behaving *like* a jerk, but *you*, Jonathan, the person, are *not* a jerk. Remember the discussion about loving yourself? You and your behavior are two different things."

"When I was trapped, I had a lot of time to think about my father and mother, my life, my friendship with Mark and Kate, and how I managed to screw up my life—*me*, not anyone else. I made everyone around me miserable with my *oh, poor me* attitude, blaming other people—mainly my father—and circumstances. Instead, I should have accepted full responsibility for my situation. I know now that was terrible, and I've been wrong about everything."

"And what now, Jonathan?"

Jonathan buried his face in his hands out of desperation and sorrow. "I want to make amends for how I have treated others, especially Kate, Mark, and you, sir. You gave me an amazing opportunity to be a part of this trip and part of your team on the dig. I know you took a big chance by letting me come along. It's been the opportunity of a lifetime, and I didn't appreciate it; I only focused on myself and what I wanted—*to be famous*. When I didn't get what I wanted, I made everyone around me miserable, threw a tantrum, and acted like a spoiled child who didn't get what he wanted in the grocery store. *I am not* that person anymore, Reverend Ken! I am not! It took a lot of thinking and writing to bring me to this place. But I know I'm not that same person anymore." The night seemed to swallow his pleading voice.

Reverend Ken looked at him but didn't speak. Jonathan continued to plead, "*I am not*! And I am sorry for my terrible behavior! In my journal, I wrote that living in the present moment, friendships, loving others, and giving more than

RECONCILIATION

taking from every relationship is the meaning of true wealth! *I'm so sorry! So, so sorry!*" Jonathan dropped to his knees, sobbing.

Reverend Hogan helped him back into his chair. Jonathan's remorse was evident, and his true heart was obvious, so the Reverend believed him. Jonathan *had* grown up a lot from this experience.

Wiping tears from his face, "How can I at least get Kate and Mark to start talking to me again?"

"You are going to have to make the initial move, Jonathan; you talked about taking responsibility—now's your chance."

Jonathan left Reverend Ken's tent and went to the ledge that had become his fortress of solitude to think and possibly write what he needed to do, worried but more determined than ever. He wrote.

> *How am I going to prove to Mark and Kate I have changed and learned a valuable lesson? How am I going to explain how sorry I am for everything? What do I say to them? What else can I say other than I'm sorry? More than that, I need to do everything I can to prove myself by not complaining but by pitching in and doing my part to finish what we started here and stop dwelling in the past—no more old Jonathan! I'm through with him!*

That evening at dinner in the cook shack, Jonathan saw Kate and Mark together, chatting and laughing. He walked over to ask if he could join them. They looked at him then at each other. After what seemed like a long pause, they responded almost in unison, "Yeah, we'd like that."

He sat across the table from them, "Thanks, I appreciate it." The conversation was uneasy at first, but soon, they talked comfortably again.

"How have your projects been going over the past couple of days?"

"Real good, we're finishing the last of the cataloging," Mark replied.

Looking at Kate with compassion in his eyes, he said, "How about you?"

"Well, I've finished the documentation. Now, I am helping my father summarize his results. We're still waiting for the results from the lab on the items we found in the underground room, but there's no question this is one of Solomon's palaces."

Momentarily, she regretted mentioning the room, and they ate silently. Jonathan poked at his food.

No one said anything about what happened between them, but finally, Jonathan broke the silence. "I've been a jerk—I know it, and I admit it. Unfortunately, I've mistreated both of you, took advantage of our friendship for many years, and acted like a spoiled brat. It is no one else's fault that I've been a miserable person and a miserable friend—no one but my own. I can't express how sorry I am for how I have behaved and treated both of you. No doubt, I've made your lives difficult with the strain my constant pity party put on our friendship. I've squandered our time together and the unconditional friendship and support you have given me for years." He placed his hands on the table as if surrendering. *I am so very, very sorry*! Can you see it in your hearts to ever forgive me?"

Both Kate and Mark were surprised by Jonathan's heartfelt expression of sorrow and honest admission of his behavior. They say the eyes are the window to the soul, and they saw the deep remorse and compassion in his eyes. Could his near-death experience really have allowed him the opportunity to reflect on his life and affect his willingness to make some changes? Only time would tell.

Kate was the first to respond, "Well, I'm glad to hear that you finally realize now how you've been behaving."

"I am so, so very sorry for everything I have said and done." Jonathan lowered his eyes.

RECONCILIATION

Mark sat open-mouthed. "Wow, it's terrific to hear you say that."

The next couple of days passed, and Jonathan acted like a different person. No one heard him complain about a single thing. He made it a point to always help because he wanted to prove himself by silently being present to offer assistance without needing acknowledgment. It was a great way to begin. Jonathan never mentioned the room again, his disappointment, his entrapment, or his near-death experience. He showed more interest than before in the dig and the final stages of the process by asking enthusiastic questions and thoroughly involving himself in what he needed to do. Genuinely, he seemed like a changed person, and everyone noticed.

The one unsettled matter was Kate's expression of feelings for him. Jonathan knew he felt a great deal for Kate but didn't know what love was supposed to feel like. His problems had consumed him, and he never gave love a chance. It felt like he needed to understand what love should be before he committed. *I don't want to hurt her any more than I already have by saying the wrong things.*

Feeling very confused, Jonathan went out into the desert again where he could think. He paced back and forth along the ledge, turning the thoughts over and over in his mind, trying to resolve the conflicted feelings he was experiencing. Once again, Jonathan felt he needed to write his thoughts down to try to make sense of what he was feeling.

> *I like Kate—I like her a lot, but she has always been more like a sister than a lover. We had a good time together over the years. There has been a lot of laughter and goofing around between us. She's smart, has so much to offer, and she's beautiful, yet I'm so ordinary. I still don't understand what she sees in me. I know—that's the old Jonathan in my head telling me I'm not good enough, and I have to keep reminding myself that it's not true.*

Scratching his head in thought, he continued.

Still, the only love I've experienced was between my parents, and if that is any way love turns out after two people get married, I don't want any part of it! On the other hand, her parents don't seem to be like that, and neither does Mark's. Not every marriage has to end up like my parents did. And maybe I am getting a little bit ahead of myself—no one has talked about marriage! I think I need to talk to Kate's dad again about this and see what he has to say.

He packed up his journal and decided to talk to Kate's father before saying anything to her about his feelings and concerns.

SEVENTEEN

TRUE WEALTH

One afternoon shortly after his reconciliation with Mark and Kate, Jonathan had completed some documentation for Reverend Ken. He decided this was the time to talk to him about Kate's feelings. Reverend Ken was in his tent, writing his research.

Jonathan approached and asked if he could speak with him again. Reverend Ken looked up from his pile of paperwork, smiled, and invited Jonathan to come in.

"Yes, certainly, please come in and have a seat. Have you completed that documentation I need?"

"Yes, sir, here it is."

"Great, thanks so much."

"It appears you've made amends with Kate and Mark."

Jonathan pulled up a chair. "Yes, sir. I'm trying to show them I have changed. Hopefully, my efforts in practicing responsibility have proven that I realize I am responsible for everything in my life. Three things really stand out for me—the value of living in the present moment, not the past, taking responsibility for my life, and the power and preciousness of true friendship. But I do have something else troubling me deeply, though, and I'm conflicted. That's what I really wanted to speak with you about."

"Yes, what is it?" Reverend Ken removed his glasses and looked up from the documents in front of him.

"Well, it's Kate and my feelings for her."

"Oh, yes. I can see that's probably a difficult situation for you considering everything that's happened."

"Yeah, for sure. I have strong feelings for Kate, but I don't know if it's love. You see, I don't think I know what love is supposed to feel like."

With that comment, Reverend Hogan smiled and chuckled.

"What's so funny?"

"Well, love is one of those mysterious emotions. It can happen suddenly—like love at first sight—all filled with passion and desire. Or love can be something that needs to be nurtured and worked on over time. Also, love comes in many different forms. I know Kate blurting out her love for you took you by surprise and shook you up a bit."

"Oh, boy, is that ever the truth!" Jonathan almost chuckled.

Reverend Hogan rested his elbows on his knees, clasped his hands, and rested his chin on his clasped hands. Jonathan thought he looked look like *The Thinker*. He pondered for a moment before speaking. "Honestly, I think you are making this too difficult on yourself. You're trying to analyze an emotion, and it is impossible. Why don't you just sit down with Kate and talk about it?"

"I'm afraid I'm going to mess it up with her or hurt her feelings again because I don't know what to say or how to say it." Jonathan felt confused and defeated.

"I don't think you're giving Kate enough credit for being understanding. She's been harboring these feelings for you for a very long time; I don't think she expects you to feel the same way she does right now. You just found this out. It's going to take some time for both of you to figure things out, and maybe never, which would be okay too. That's the way it should be. It's not a do-or-die situation."

"But Kate was all *I've loved you since the sixth grade,* crying and stuff!"

"She allowed a harbored emotion she's kept secret for years to come out all at once. I think she realized it was the wrong way to go about letting you know her feelings."

"Okay, so once again, you think it's all right to take this relationship thing slow and easy with Kate?"

"Yes, I do. Talk to her, Jonathan."

Okay, I'll do that and cross my fingers."

"Also, I have another matter I need to discuss with you, Jonathan."

Oh, man, what have I done now? Jonathan thought, but instead, he said, "What is it, sir?"

"How do you feel about archaeology?"

"Huh? What do you mean?"

"Do you like digging around in the dirt and exploring the past? You appear to have a natural aptitude for it, an analytical mind, and an innate curiosity."

"Well, I like it very much. It's like solving a big puzzle and finding clues that have been hidden for centuries. And I've always enjoyed puzzles, and my mom reminded me how gifted I was at them. Alternatively, I always hated history in school; it was so dull reading about old stuff in a book, but being here, hands-on involved in uncovering history was entirely different. Being in this ancient place and discovering how people lived hundreds or even thousands of years ago fascinates me! Jonathan's eyes brightened, and he sat forward. It was so exciting when I found a pottery sherd with markings on it—it looked similar to one I found the day before, and I could piece them together. It told a story about real people and how they lived. Why do you ask?"

Reverend Hogan smiled over Jonathan's excitement.

"Well, I've discovered a new opportunity, but first, I needed to know how you felt about archaeology. It sounds like you enjoy the field, so how would you feel about studying to be an archaeologist?"

"What? Who, me?"

"You have an opportunity to go to college and study archaeology. That is, if you want it!"

"What are you saying? What do you mean?"

"It means you have a full paid scholarship to go to college and study to be an archaeologist if you want to. *That's what it means!*"

Jonathan's jaw dropped. "What?! How is this? What the? I can't believe it! How is this possible? I dropped out of high school, and my grades were lousy. Honestly, I had to get a GED, and I'm dyslexic! How would any college accept me?"

"Listen, you think your dyslexia is a handicap, that somehow you are broken. It isn't! Did you know that many famous people had dyslexia?"

Jonathan lifted an eyebrow. "Who?"

Reverend Ken put his hand on Jonathan's shoulder. "Gosh. Well, George Washington, Thomas Edison, Henry Ford, Albert Einstein, Leonardo da Vinci, and Pablo Picasso, just to name a few. Look it up if you don't believe me! You aren't *defective; you aren't a reject* because you have dyslexia! I've noticed your interest in archaeology seemed to blossom, and frankly, you've seemed to come alive here. So, I decided to look into college on your behalf because I think one thing you lacked was your teachers' support, and your grades aren't as bad as you assumed. Besides, there are tools and computer programs designed to assist students with learning disabilities now that didn't exist when you were in school. You'd begin the year on academic probation. Then, after that, they'll reinstate you if you keep your grades up."

Reverend Hogan took a sip of his coffee. "I have a close friend who happens to be the Dean of the Archaeology Department at the University of Missouri. He looked at your academic records and is willing to consider you as a candidate for their program. Also, it appears you have friends in high places in the Israeli government who have taken an interest in you. I know you've struggled, Jonathan, but I've noted your keen eye for this type of work and attention to detail, and the Israelis would like you to return to Jerusalem during the summers to intern at the Israel Antiquities Authority."

Jonathan hadn't closed his mouth since Reverend Ken started speaking. He stammered, "I, I can't believe this! It's too incredible for me even to comprehend! Why me?"

"You instinctively uncovered the staircase that led to one of the most significant archeological discoveries in history! You not only verified this site as one of Solomon's palaces, but you gave the archaeological community answers to many questions regarding this period in Middle Eastern history. You're famous in archaeological circles! I don't think you realize how monumental your discovery was, Jonathan. It didn't surprise me that the Israeli government wanted to have someone like you working with them. As I said, you have a natural aptitude and instinct for archaeology! All this is true if you want it. I can handle the arrangements if you say yes."

"Yes, yes, yes! Oh my gosh, *yes*!"

"Good, I'll let the Dean know your decision. After we return home, you'll leave two weeks later, so we'll need to make preparations soon. Also, I spoke with my wife, and we'd like to invite you to stay in the guest suite above our garage until it is time to leave."

"Reverend Ken, how can I *possibly* ever repay you? I can't thank you enough for this opportunity."

"You can get good grades and prove to *yourself* that you can do anything you set your mind on doing, son! That's how you can repay me."

"I won't let you down, sir! I won't let you down! I promise!"

"You won't be letting me down; you'd be letting yourself down. Now, get out of here and go to tell your friends your good news!"

Jonathan thanked him again, grabbed his bag, and started to rush out of the tent. But in the process, he knocked over a stack of papers on the edge of the desk.

"Oh my gosh, I am so sorry." As he gathered and straightened the papers and put them back on the desk, Reverend Hogan smiled, shook his head, put his glasses on, and returned to his paperwork as Jonathan disappeared in a cloud of dust to find Kate and Mark.

A short while later, Jonathan found Kate working alone and asked her if she would walk with him. "Sure. Give me a couple of minutes to finish this up. He nervously paced back and forth while he waited as she finished what she was doing. "There. What's on your mind?"

As they walked off together, Jonathan offered another apology. "Kate, I can't tell you how truly sorry I am for speaking to you the way I did. My behavior was uncalled for, and I am deeply sorry."

He continued, "Your declaration of love surprised me. I didn't know how to react to your feelings; out of habit, I responded harshly without thinking. When you jumped up and kissed me and said you loved me, I didn't know what to think. *Frankly, I freaked out*! Forgive me. I'm sorry I didn't know how to deal with someone—especially you—telling me they loved me."

"I think I need to apologize, too, for jumping up and kissing you—that was impulsive. After it happened, I knew it was the wrong way to express my feelings. But why was it such a shock?"

"Well, it was *you*! I've known you practically my whole life, and we're like, friends and stuff."

"So, do you know how to deal with my feelings now?" she asked, smiling.

"I don't know. Loving someone is a new experience, but I think I'm better now than I was at the time."

"What does that mean?"

"It means I'd like to take it slowly—if that's okay with you—and see where it takes both of us. I care a great deal for you, a lot more than I realized. I've had time to understand what is important in life and how important love can be. I've done a lot of growing up the past few weeks."

Kate smiled at him, took his hand, and said, "I have waited a long time to hear you say that. That's all I need right now." She stood on her tiptoes and kissed him on the cheek as her hair tickled his face. He smiled and hugged her tenderly.

"Now, I have some great news to share with you, but we need to find Mark first." She grabbed his hand and squeezed it gently. Jonathan felt a warm tingling spread up his arm as they held hands on their walk to find Mark.

"Can't you tell me what this is all about?" Kate asked.

"Nope! I'll tell you all the news, but we need to find Mark first."

"I don't think I've seen you excited like this about anything in years."

"For the first time in a long time, I have something to *be* excited about!"

They found Mark sitting in the shade of one of the tents, and when he saw them, he looked perplexed.

"What's wrong with you?" Kate asked.

"Well, well, well! It looks like the two of you have managed to iron things out!"

They had forgotten they were still holding hands. "Yes, *Mr. Smarty-Pants*, we have!" Kate replied as she held their hands up.

"I've got some fantastic news I'd like to share with you guys!" Jonathan blurted out.

"Yes, please tell us. I am about to explode, waiting to find out what has happened!" Kate exclaimed.

"Okay! *Mr. Smarty-Pants* is always ready for some fantastic news. Welcome to my humble shade. Pull up a chair and give us your fantastic news, *oh fantastic news giver,*" Mark said with his well-known bravado as he leaned back in his chair.

Well, he's back in rare form. Jonathan thought as he and Kate pulled up chairs as if they were going to share a big secret like they did when they were kids.

"Well, I just left Reverend Ken's tent a little while ago. He had something he wanted to talk to me about."

"Okay, don't keep us in suspense; spill it. I'm sitting on pins and needles here." Mark playfully punched Jonathan's arm.

"Give him a chance, Mark. But please don't keep us in suspense any longer!" Kate chimed in.

"Alright, alright, already, I'll shut up and listen." Mark laughed.

"He asked me how I felt about archaeology," Jonathan told them.

"Huh? *How do you feel about archaeology?* That's a weird question," Mark interjected. Kate rolled her eyes—Mark's cue to be quiet—and let Jonathan tell his news.

"Yeah, he wanted to know how I liked digging in the dirt and exploring the past."

"Ah, the plot thickens!"

"Mark, if you don't stop it, I'm gonna!" Jonathan smiled as he made a fist.

"Okay, *okay*!"

"Well, I told him I liked it a lot. I've learned a bunch of cool stuff on this trip."

"Oh, yeah, and *gett'n yourself trapped in an underground room.* Not to mention, almost dying." Mark chuckled.

Kate playfully slapped him on the arm. "Stop it!"

He feigned injury and pretended to protect himself. "Well, it's true!"

Jonathan rolled his eyes at their playful banter. "If I may continue?" Mark nodded in agreement. Kate gave him a cross look and smiled.

"The reason your dad asked me all those questions about archaeology and my interest in digging in the dirt was . . . can I have a drum roll, Mark?"

With imaginary drumsticks in his hands flailing around like he was playing drums, Mark obliged. "Ta-Daaa!"

"Kate, your father, along with the Israeli government, have managed to get me a full paid scholarship to the University of Missouri to study archaeology! I leave two weeks after we return home!"

Mark and Kate sat open-mouthed and speechless. For Jonathan, it felt like an eternity as they looked at him, stunned. He wondered if they were happy for him.

In unison, "What! *Shut up!*"

Then, they both jumped at the same time, rushed him with hugs and kisses, and knocked him backward in his chair. The three rolled around on the ground; Mark and Kate hugged him, tousled his hair, and laughed and cried with joy and excitement. At that moment, the three of them were eight years old again.

"Oh, Jon, that *is* the most fantastic news!" Kate cheered.

"Hey, buddy, that *is* fantastic news! You're going to go for it, aren't you?" Mark asked.

"Absolutely! This is the best thing that has ever happened to me."

"I'm so happy for you! And I think you'll make an incredible archaeologist!"

"I do too. How can we celebrate?" Mark asked.

"Oh, well, I guess we can help ourselves to an extra piece of *mystery meat* at dinner tonight!" Jonathan said with a grin as the three of them laughed, sitting there in the dirt.

"That sounds great to me! I'm always up for food," Mark replied.

Kate shook her head and rolled her eyes. "You *are* disgusting!"

EIGHTEEN

RETURN AND DEFEAT OF THE SHADOWS

That night, it was impossible for Jonathan to sleep. It felt like every cell in his body was vibrating with excitement. He knew that he needed to write this down so he could reread and experience the feelings all over again.

I think that today was the most fantastic day of my life! Three wonderful things happened. First, Kate and I agreed to take our blossoming relationship one day at a time so that each of us can discover how we actually feel about the other. I'm feeling awkward and confused right now, and she is willing to let me figure things out between us. The one thing I can say for sure is I like the feeling a lot!

Second, I received the most generous offer I have ever gotten in my whole and entire life—a full scholarship to go to college and study archaeology! So I'm not a reject after all! It took other people seeing my value and skills to make me see them. And now that I do, I can develop my skills. Reverend Ken believes I'll make a great archaeologist. No one has ever had any faith in me before. No one has ever given me a chance, and now I have one. I actually feel like I can do this!

And three, I have my two best friends back. And this time, I'm going to treasure that relationship and put more into it than I ask from it. Mark and Kate have been great at sticking with me through my dark time and wanted to genuinely help me, but I was too blinded by my ignorance to understand what they kept telling me. I treated them terribly, mainly Kate. How could I have been so blind not to see love right under my nose?

My biggest realization is that I have always had the capabilities to do, be, or have anything I wanted. I allowed other people or circumstances to cause me to believe otherwise. I don't need to do something special to be someone special. I have always been extraordinary!

The next few days passed very quickly as the dig team wrapped up preparations to return home. Meanwhile, the Israeli team members prepared to return to their homes and schools. The team made a lot of friendships during this time, living and working together. Everyone grew in many ways. News of Jonathan's good fortune spread throughout the camp, and everyone was excited about his opportunity to attend college and return to Isreal for his internship.

Those who witnessed his outburst following the initial discovery had moved on and forgiven him for his childish behavior when they saw his changed attitude. Though they were shocked and surprised at the time, the whole story about Jonathan's history surfaced as time passed. Interestingly, even though Jonathan initially came on the trip hoping to become famous, he became a bit of a celebrity when other people learned about his part in the discovery. However, now he shunned the notoriety and chuckled to realize that fame was not at all what he really wanted or needed now. He had discovered the value of himself. Instead, he smiled and thanked them. Jonathan smiled a lot of the time now.

The U.S. team packed everything and got ready to return home from their memorable adventure; a lot had happened in the two months, more than any of them could have anticipated. They had made a significant archaeological discovery to benefit scientific, historical, and religious scholars for years to come. Their findings—contents of the storage jars, new information about people's diets, and scrolls found in the sealed containers—all provided information on commerce and life three thousand years ago. The inscriptions and seals found in the room confirmed that the ancient site was one of King Solomon's palaces.

Before they broke camp and went their separate ways, Reverend Hogan spoke to the assembled group, "This has been an incredible trip for me. I have all of you to thank for this amazing adventure. Thank you all so very much! We've made some monumental discoveries; some will take scientists and historians years to unravel. I am very proud of each of you, and again, thank you from the bottom of my heart! Goodbye and Shalom!" Rousing applause erupted from the entire dig team as he playfully bowed and raised his arms in a symbol of victory.

"I can't believe it's coming to an end. The time has flown by so quickly," Jonathan said.

"Don't worry. It sounds like it won't be long before you are back here again."

"I know. This trip has changed my life forever. It's difficult for me to see it end. The old me died in these ruins, but at the same time, I found myself and discovered the meaning of true wealth."

"*Please* don't use that word. Let's not talk about dying—if you don't mind," Kate interjected.

As he pretended to take a big bite of something, he said, "Well, I'll be glad to get back home and have a burger and fries from the Northside Drive-in and their chocolate shake!" Mark rubbed his stomach.

"Oh, you are always thinking about food," Kate added with a laugh.

"Well, let's face it. The food on this trip hasn't been worth writing home about!"

"Agreed!" in unison.

The trip back home was anticlimactic for Jonathan. He was not the same person who left two months before. After seeing another part of the world, his feelings about Harrington weren't the same. He still loved his quiet hometown and its familiarity. The *now-Jonathan* had Kate, and Reverend Ken had become almost like a father to him. Of course, he still had his best friend, Mark. But now, there were other opportunities and options for his life; he never realized he could consider those things before.

Jonathan pondered the past two months as he watched Jerusalem and the Holy Land disappear outside the airplane window. While the others dozed, Jonathan took the time to write down his thoughts.

> *I could never have believed my life could change so dramatically in just eight weeks. When I left Harrington, I was a miserable, self-centered person. I thought outside circumstances would make my life better. But if I want things to change, then I have to change my thoughts first, which permits all kinds of amazing things to happen.*
>
> *I wonder where Jedidiah is now. Why didn't I get a chance to see him again after the hospital? Who was he? Will I ever see him again?*

RETURN AND DEFEAT OF THE SHADOWS

On the van ride from the Albany airport to Harrington, Jonathan looked out the window at the green countryside. He remembered two short months ago and remarked to Kate, "Look how green and lush everything is in comparison to the desert. What an unbelievable contrast. Like the difference in my life then and now."

"You miss the desert, don't you?"

"The desert? Yes, I do; it's an amazing place. But now, it's time to move forward, and that's what I intend to do. There are a lot more adventures ahead."

In the meantime, news of the discovery and the events in Israel had reached home. It caused a lot of excitement in town. When the dig team arrived at the church to unpack their gear and reunite with their families, many people waited to greet them.

Jonathan was with Kate, Reverend Hogan, Mark, and the other dig team members unloading their equipment from the van. There was lots of excitement and experiences to share as families reunited. Jonathan saw a lot of hugging, shaking hands, warm welcomes home, and tears of joy. Mrs. Hogan ran up and gave her husband and Kate big hugs. Mark's parents were there to welcome him back with a burger and fries. "We figured you'd want these!" They laughed. Mark's parents greeted Jonathan with a hug and a handshake. "Welcome back! You've become a bit of a celebrity." When they noticed Kate and Jonathan held hands, Mr. Atkins said, "It appears you found something else while in the desert too."

Jonathan and Kate smiled as Mrs. Hogan gave her husband a surprised look. But he feigned innocence.

Suddenly, they saw Jonathan's father pushing his way through the crowd toward them.

Mark whispered in Jonathan's ear, "What's *he* doing here?"

"I don't have the faintest idea."

Pete came up to Jonathan, grabbed him, and gave his son a big hug. He stepped back with a big smile on his face holding Jonathan's shoulders. "And here's my famous archaeologist son! Welcome home, Jonathan. It's so good to have you back. The whole town knew you discovered that old stuff! I'm so proud of you!"

Judging by the looks on the others' faces, they were all shocked, particularly Jonathan. "Hey, why don't we head for home and get out of this crowd? I imagine you have a lot to tell me about your adventure. Your room upstairs is all ready."

Jonathan looked at his father, surprised. "Well, thanks anyway. But I'm *not* famous, just part of the dig team. And I'm *not* an archaeologist yet. Also, Reverend Hogan is letting me stay with them for a couple of weeks before I leave."

Pete asked, "Leave? Where are you going now?"

"I'm leaving for college in two weeks."

"College! Where? How are *you* going to go to college?"

"The University of Missouri. Reverend Hogan and the Israeli government arranged it for me. Reverend Hogan said I have a natural aptitude and the curiosity it takes to make a great archaeologist. I've found something I really love doing, and I'm good at it."

Pete shot an angry glance at Reverend Hogan and replied sarcastically, "Well, good luck with that! You're going to need all the help you can get!"

Jonathan calmly responded, "Dad, I don't need any help. I'm doing this because I know I can."

With that, Pete turned and pushed his way through the crowd. As he left, he mumbled one last time, "Loser!"

Reverend Hogan put his hand on Jonathan's shoulder as Jonathan gently squeezed Kate's hand. He smiled as he watched his father melt back into the excited crowd. He felt peace in a way he never had before. He finally felt like he found a place to belong. His path was ahead of him, and it didn't matter what his father said. Jonathan was going to blaze his own trail for a bright future.

A NOTE FROM THE AUTHOR

> Truth is within ourselves; it takes no rise
> From outward things, whate'er you may believe.
> There is an inmost center in us all
> Where truth abides in fullness. . .
> —Robert Browning

Writing this story has been a labor of love for me and cathartic. Even now, many years later, sometimes I still struggle with those voices in my head that tell me I'm not enough, not deserving, and lazy.

I believe it is safe to say that millions of people live plagued by their histories—unconscious programming from childhood onward. Most of this programming is well-intentioned, though sometimes delivered in anger or frustration by influential people or by mean or thoughtless children on the playground. This programming can be verbal or non-verbal, a look or body language, indicating the withdrawal of love or acceptance.

Most relate to terms from childhood: "You're a bad boy." "Young ladies don't behave like that." "You're a spoiled, selfish child." "You're so stupid." "Why can't you do anything right?" "You're lazy." "Ew, do we have to have you on our team?" There are countless terrible nicknames we may have lived with because of our physical appearance or physical inabilities. And we still listen to them many years later.

> *We become what we think about most of the time, and that's the strangest secret.*
> —Earl Nightingale

Here is a pertinent statistic. Benjamin Hardy, Ph.D., wrote in his article appearing in Medium.org, *To Have What You Want, You Must Give-Up What's Holding You Back*, June 9, 2018, "In 2005, According to the National Science Foundation, an average person has about 12,000 to 60,000 thoughts per day. Of those, 80% are negative, and 95% are exactly the same repetitive thoughts as the day before." If we repeat those negative thoughts, we think negatively way more than we think positively. It is not surprising that so many of us feel unfulfilled and lacking in our lives.

Part of the human spirit desperately wants to feel connected, necessary in some way, and valued by someone. Still, we get in our own way more often than not due to these insidious lies we keep telling ourselves.

Unfortunately, because we have lived with these lies, we have allowed them to become a part of our self-image. They have become habits that cause us to think, act, and live lives of quiet desperation, tiptoeing by, hoping to make it safely to death.

Although we grow up with this negative programming, it is crucial to realize that it is possible to change our thinking and the direction of our lives.

The way to true wealth is much more than obtaining money, although money can certainly be part of it. The journey begins by realizing that no matter what type of negative programming you faced, one thing remains forever valid: **You are a magnificent being created by God and perfect in every way.** Some would have you believe otherwise, but this fact is irrefutable. God does not make mistakes! You came into this

A NOTE FROM THE AUTHOR

world a perfect creation with unlimited potential and are in control of your life and your choices—wealth, success, vibrant health, loving relationships, joy, and a sense of connection to everything that originates as our thoughts. Indeed, thoughts do become things. Your challenge is to decide which ideas you allow yourself to think about regularly. Are they positive, uplifting, and encouraging, or negative, downgrading, and depressing? Remember the statistics above.

I give *Solomon's Riches* to you in the hope that you will recognize some aspect of yourself and your history in this story. Then, use the newfound wisdom (true wealth) to realize your magnificence and choose to make some changes in your life and thinking.

With much love,
Steve Darr
March 2021
Steve@SteveDarr.com

ACKNOWLEDGMENTS

I would like to thank Kary Oberbrunner and all of the people from Author Academy Elite and the Igniting Souls tribe for their support and encouragement. A very special thank you to my editor, Felicity Fox, for her guidance, insight, and belief in this story to help me bring it to life. To Tina Morlock, the managing editor at Author Academy, who oversaw the editing process. Thank you, Debbie O'Byrne, for the beautiful cover design of the book and all the other designers and people from JetLaunch who, with their incredible help, made this story a physical reality. Many thanks to Ann Williams, my proofreader, who kindly lent another set of eyes to the final manuscript. And especially my life partner and spouse, David, who supported me in this endeavor as he always has.

On a personal note, thank you, Bob Proctor, for your programs, seminars, and many years of insightful wisdom. I have enjoyed watching and listening to you. I am the better for it. And thanks to Peggy McColl for her programs, through which I have gained much knowledge and insight. To Earnest Holmes, whose writings gave me my first understanding of my intimate connection with God and my inner magnificence. To Mike Dooley, who helped me realize that we all possess infinite possibilities. And to the many authors and teachers, living and dead, for their insights into spiritual wisdom, psychology, and the human experience. They have all added to my ability to better understand myself and my way to true wealth.

Last, but not least, Jessica Brody for her novel writing class Writing a Bestselling Novel in 15 Steps (Writing Mastery), and book, *Save the Cat Writes a Novel*. My guidebook for writing this, my first novel. May there be many more to follow.

Thank you all!

Our lives are but specks of dust
Falling through the fingers of time.
Like sands of the hourglass, so are the days of our lives.
—Socrates

RESOURCES

PROGRAMS

SPEAKING

DOWNLOADS

Visit my website
www.SteveDarr.com
steve@stevedarr.com

www.ingramcontent.com/pod-product-compliance
Lightning Source LLC
LaVergne TN
LVHW041637060526
838200LV00040B/1601

9 781647 467777